Imm

IMMORTALITY INC.

Robert Sheckley

A LEGEND BOOK

Published by Arrow Books Limited
20 Vauxhall Bridge Road, London SW1V 2SA

An imprint of the Random Century Group

London Melbourne Sydney Auckland
Johannesburg and agencies throughout
the world

Century/Legend edition 1992

This Arrow/Legend edition 1992

1 3 5 7 9 10 8 6 4 2

Printed and bound in Great Britain by
Cox & Wyman Ltd, Reading, Berkshire

ISBN 0 09 15741 1

PART ONE

1

Afterwards, Thomas Blaine thought about the manner of his dying and wished it had been more interesting. Why couldn't his death have come while he was battling a typhoon, meeting a tiger's charge, or climbing a windswept mountain? Why had his death been so tame, so commonplace, so ordinary?

But an enterprising death, he realized, would have been out of character for him. Undoubtedly he was meant to die in just the quick, common, messy, painless way he did. And all his life must have gone into the forming and shaping of that death – a vague indication in childhood, a fair promise in his college years, an implacable certainty at the age of thirty-two.

Still, no matter how commonplace, one's death is the most interesting event of one's life. Blaine thought about his with intense curiosity. He had to know about those minutes, those last precious seconds when his own particular death lay waiting for him on a dark New Jersey highway. Had there been some warning sign, some portent? What had he done, or not done? What had he been thinking?

Those final seconds were crucial to him. How, exactly, had he died?

He had been driving over a straight, empty white highway, his headlights probing ahead, the darkness receding endlessly before him. His speedometer read seventy-five. It felt like forty. Far down the road he saw headlights coming toward him, the first in hours.

Blaine was returning to New York after a week's vacation at his cabin on Chesapeake Bay. He had fished and swum and dozed in the sun on the rough planks of his dock. One day he sailed his sloop to Oxford and attended a dance at the yacht club that night. He met a silly, pert-nosed girl in a blue dress who told him he looked like a South Seas adventurer, so tanned and tall in his khakis. He sailed back to his cabin the next day, to doze in the sun and dream of giving up everything, loading his sailboat with canned goods and heading for Tahiti. *Ah Raïatea, the mountains of Mooréa, the fresh trade wind . . .*

But a continent and an ocean lay between him and Tahiti, and other obstacles besides. The thought was only for an hour's dreaming, and definitely not to be acted upon. Now he was returning to New York, to his job as a junior yacht designer for the famous old firm of Mattison & Peters.

The other car's headlights were drawing near. Blaine slowed to sixty.

In spite of his title, there were few yachts for Blaine to design. Old Tom Mattison took care of the conventional cruising boats. His brother Rolf, known as the Wizard of Mystic, had an international reputation for his ocean-racing sailboats and fast one-designs. So what was there for a junior yacht designer to do?

Blaine drew layouts and deck plans, and handled promotion, advertising and publicity. It was responsible work, and not without its satisfactions. But it was not yacht designing.

He knew he should strike out on his own. But there were so many yacht designers, so few customers. As he had told Laura, it was rather like designing arbalests, scorpions and catapults. Interesting creative work, but who would buy your products?

'You could find a market for your sailboats,' she had told him, distressingly direct. 'Why not make the plunge?'

He had grinned boyishly, charmingly. 'Action isn't my forte. I'm an expert on contemplation and mild regret.'

'You mean you're lazy.'

'Not at all. That's like saying that a hawk doesn't gallop well, or a horse has poor soaring ability. You can't compare different species. I'm just not the go-getter type of human. For me, dreams, reveries, visions, and plans are meant only for contemplation, never for execution.'

'I hate to hear you talk like that,' she said with a sigh.

4

He *had* been laying it on a bit thick, of course. But there was a lot of truth in it. He had a pleasant job, an adequate salary, a secure position. He had an apartment in Greenwich Village, a hi-fi, a car, a small cabin on Chesapeake Bay, a fine sloop, and the affection of Laura and several other girls. Perhaps, as Laura somewhat tritely expressed it, he was caught in an eddy on the current of life . . . But so what? You could observe the scenery better from a gently revolving eddy.

The other car's headlights were very near. Blaine noticed, with a sense of shock, that he had increased speed to eighty miles an hour.

He let up on the accelerator. His car swerved freakishly, violently, toward the oncoming headlights.

Blowout? Steering failure? He twisted hard on the steering wheel. It wouldn't turn. His car struck the low concrete separation between north and south lanes, and bounded high into the air. The steering wheel came free and spun in his hands, and the engine wailed like a lost soul.

The other car was trying to swerve, too late. They were going to meet nearly head-on.

And Blaine thought, yes, I'm one of them. I'm one of those silly bastards you read about whose cars go out of control and kill innocent people. Christ! Modern cars and modern roads and higher speeds and the same old sloppy reflexes . . .

Suddenly, unaccountably, the steering wheel was working again, a razor's edge reprieve. Blaine ignored it. As the other car's headlights glared across his windshield, his mood suddenly changed from regret to exultance. For a moment he welcomed the smash, lusted for it, and for pain, destruction, cruelty and death.

Then the cars came together. The feeling of exultance faded as quickly as it had come. Blaine felt a profound regret for all he had left undone, the waters unsailed, movies unseen, books unread, girls untouched. He was thrown forward. The steering wheel broke off in his hands. The steering column speared him through the chest and broke his spine as his head drove through the thick safety glass.

At that instant he knew he was dying.

An instant later he was quickly, commonly, messily, painlessly dead.

2

He awoke in a white bed in a white room.

'He's alive now,' someone said.

Blaine opened his eyes. Two men in white were standing over him. They seemed to be doctors. One was a small, bearded old man. The other was an ugly red-faced man in his fifties.

'What's your name?' the old man snapped.

'Thomas Blaine.'

'Age?'

'Thirty-two. But –'

'Marital status?'

'Single. What –'

'Do you see?' the old man said, turning to his red-faced colleague. 'Sane, perfectly sane.'

'I would never have believed it,' said the red-faced man.

'But of course. The death trauma has been overrated. Grossly overrated, as my forthcoming book will prove.'

'Hmm. But rebirth depression –'

'Nonsense,' the old man said decisively. 'Blaine, do you feel all right?'

'Yes. But I'd like to know –'

'Do you see?' the old doctor said triumphantly. 'Alive again and sane. *Now* will you co-sign the report?'

'I suppose I have no choice,' the red-faced man said. Both doctors left.

Blaine watched them go, wondering what they had been talking about. A fat and motherly nurse came to his bedside. 'How do you feel?' she asked.

'Fine,' Blaine said. 'But I'd like to know –'

'Sorry,' the nurse said, 'no questions yet, doctor's orders. Drink this, it'll pep you up. That's a good boy. Don't worry, everything's going to be all right.'

She left. Her reassuring words frightened him. What did

she mean, *everything's going to be all right*? That meant something was wrong! What was it, what was wrong? What was he doing here, what had happened?

The bearded doctor returned, accompanied by a young woman.

'Is he all right, doctor?' the young woman asked.

'Perfectly sane,' the old doctor said. 'I'd call it a good splice.'

'Then I can begin the interview?'

'Certainly. Though I cannot guarantee his behavior. The death trauma, though grossly overrated, is still capable of –'

'Yes, fine.' The girl walked over to Blaine and bent over him. She was a very pretty girl, Blaine noticed. Her features were clean-cut, her skin fresh and glowing. She had long, gleaming brown hair pulled too tightly back over her small ears, and there was a faint hint of perfume about her. She should have been beautiful; but she was marred by the immobility of her features, the controlled tenseness of her slender body. It was hard to imagine her laughing or crying. It was impossible to imagine her in bed. There was something of the fanatic about her, of the dedicated revolutionary; but he suspected that her cause was herself.

'Hello, Mr. Blaine,' she said. 'I'm Marie Thorne.'

'Hello,' Blaine said cheerfully.

'Mr. Blaine,' she said, 'where do you suppose you are?'

'Looks like a hospital. I suppose –' He stopped. He had just noticed a small microphone in her hand.

'Yes, what do you suppose?'

She made a small gesture. Men came forward and wheeled heavy equipment around his bed.

'Go right ahead,' Marie Thorne said. 'Tell us what you suppose.'

'To hell with that,' Blaine said moodily, watching the men set up their machines around him. 'What is this? What is going on?'

'We're trying to help you,' Marie Thorne said. 'Won't you cooperate?'

Blaine nodded, wishing she would smile. He suddenly felt very unsure of himself. Had something happened to him?

8

'Do you remember the accident?' she asked.

'What accident?'

'Do you remember being hurt?'

Blaine shuddered as his memory returned in a rush of spinning lights, wailing engine, impact and breakage.

'Yes. The steering wheel broke. I got it through the chest. Then my head hit.'

'Look at your chest,' she said softly.

Blaine looked. His chest, beneath white pajamas, was unmarked.

'Impossible!' he cried. His own voice sounded hollow, distant, unreal. He was aware of the men around his bed talking as they bent over their machines, but they seemed like shadows, flat and without substance. Their thin, unimportant voices were like flies buzzing against a window.

'Nice first reaction.'

'Very nice indeed.'

Marie Thorne said to him, 'You are unhurt.'

Blaine looked at his undamaged body and remembered the accident. 'I can't believe it!' he cried.

'He's coming on perfectly.'

'Fine mixture of belief and incredulity.'

Marie Thorne said, 'Quiet, please. Go ahead, Mr. Blaine.'

'I remember the accident,' Blaine said. 'I remember the smashing, I remember – dying.'

'Get that?'

'Hell, yes. It really plays!'

'Perfectly spontaneous scene.'

'Marvellous! They'll go wild over it!'

She said, 'A little less noise, please. Mr. Blaine, do you remember dying?'

'Yes, yes, I died!'

'His face!'

'That ludicrous expression heightens the reality.'

'I just hope Reilly thinks so.'

She said, 'Look carefully at your body, Mr. Blaine. Here's a mirror. Look at your face.'

Blaine looked, and shivered like a man in fever. He touched the mirror, then ran shaking fingers over his face.

'It isn't my face! Where's my face? Where did you put my body and face?'

He was in a nightmare from which he could never awaken. The flat shadow men surrounded him, their voices buzzing like flies against a window, tending their cardboard machines, filled with vague menace, yet strangely indifferent, almost unaware of him. Marie Thorne bent low over him with her pretty, blank face, and from her small red mouth came gentle nightmare words.

'Your body is dead, Mr. Blaine, killed in an automobile accident. You can remember its dying. But we managed to save that part of you that really counts. We saved your mind, Mr. Blaine, and have given you a new body for it.'

Blaine opened his mouth to scream, and closed it again. 'It's unbelievable,' he said quietly.

And the flies buzzed.

'*Understatement.*'

'*Well, of course. One can't be frenetic forever.*'

'*I expected a little more scenery-chewing.*'

'*Wrongly. Understatement rather accentuates his dilemma.*'

'*Perhaps, in pure stage terms. But consider the thing realistically. This poor bastard has just discovered that he died in an automobile accident and is now reborn in a new body. So what does he say about it? He says, "It's unbelievable." Damn it, he's not really reacting to the shock!*'

'*He is! You're projecting!*'

'Please!' Marie Thorne said. 'Go on, Mr. Blaine.'

Blaine, deep in his nightmare, was hardly aware of the soft, buzzing voices. He asked, 'Did I really die?'

She nodded.

'And I am really born again in a different body?'

She nodded again, waiting.

Blaine looked at her, and at the shadow men tending their cardboard machines. Why were they bothering him? Why couldn't they go pick on some other dead man? Corpses shouldn't be forced to answer questions. Death was a man's ancient privilege, his immemorial pact with life, granted to

10

the slave as well as the noble. Death was man's solace, and his right. But perhaps they had revoked that right; and now you couldn't evade your responsibilities simply by being dead.

They were waiting for him to speak. And Blaine wondered if insanity still retained its hereditary privileges. With ease he could slip over and find out.

But insanity is not granted to everyone. Blaine's self-control returned. He looked up at Marie Thorne.

'My feelings,' he said slowly, 'are difficult to describe. I've died, and now I'm contemplating the fact. I don't suppose any man fully believes in his own death. Deep down he feels immortal. Death seems to await others, but never oneself. It's almost as though –'

'*Let's cut it right here. He's getting analytical.*'

'I think you're right,' Marie Thorne said. 'Thank you very much, Mr. Blaine.'

The men, solid and mundane now, their vague menace disappeared, began rolling their equipment.

'Wait –' Blaine said.

'Don't worry,' she told him. 'We'll get the rest of your reactions later. We just wanted to record the spontaneous part now.'

'*Damn good while it lasted.*'

'*A collector's item.*'

'Wait!' Blaine cried. 'I don't understand. Where am I? What happened? How –'

'I'll explain everything tomorrow,' Marie Thorne said. 'I'm terribly sorry, I must hurry now and edit this for Mr. Reilly.'

The men and equipment were gone. Marie Thorne smiled reassuringly, and hurried away.

Blaine felt ridiculously close to tears. He blinked rapidly when the fat and motherly nurse came back.

'Drink this,' said the nurse. 'It'll make you sleep. That's it, take it all down like a good boy. Just relax, you had a big day, what with dying and being reborn and all.'

Two big tears rolled down Blaine's cheeks.

'Dear me, said the nurse, 'the cameras should be here

now. Those are genuine spontaneous tears if ever I saw any. Many a tragic and spontaneous scene I've witnessed in this infirmary, believe me, and I could tell those snooty recording boys something about genuine emotion if I wanted to, and they thinking they know all the secrets of the human heart.'

'Where am I?' Blaine asked drowsily. 'Where is this?'

'You'd call it being in the future,' the nurse said.

'Oh,' said Blaine.

Then he was asleep.

3

After many hours he awoke, calm and rested. He looked at the white bed and white room, and remembered.

He had been killed in an accident and reborn in the future. There had been a doctor who considered the death trauma overrated, and men who recorded his spontaneous reactions and declared them a collector's item, and a pretty girl whose features showed a lamentable lack of emotion.

Blaine yawned and stretched. Dead. Dead at thirty-two. A pity, he thought, that this young life was snuffed in its prime. Blaine was a good sort, really, and quite promising . . .

He was annoyed at his flippant attitude. It was no way to react. He tried to recapture the shock he felt he should feel.

Yesterday, he told himself firmly, I was a yacht designer driving back from Maryland. Today I am a man reborn into the future. The future! Reborn!

No use, the words lacked impact. He had already grown used to the idea. One grows used to anything, he thought, even to one's death. *Especially* to one's death. You could probably chop off a man's head three times a day for twenty years and he'd grow used to it, and cry like a baby if you stopped . . .

He didn't care to pursue that train of thought any further.

He thought about Laura. Would she weep for him? Would she get drunk? Or would she just feel depressed at the news, and take a tranquillizer for it? What about Jane and Miriam? Would they even hear about his death? Probably not. Months later they might wonder why he never called any more.

Enough of that. All that was past. Now he was in the *future*.

But all he had seen of the future was a white bed and a

13

white room, doctors and a nurse, recording men and a pretty girl. So far, it didn't offer much contrast with his own age. But doubtless there were differences.

He remembered magazine articles and stories he had read. Today there might be free atomic power, undersea farming, world peace, international birth control, interplanetary travel, free love, complete desegregation, a cure for all diseases, and a planned society in which men breathed deep the air of freedom.

That's what there should be, Blaine thought. But there were less pleasant possibilities. Perhaps a grim-faced Oligarch had Earth in his iron grasp, while a small, dedicated underground struggled toward freedom. Or small, gelatinous alien creatures with outlandish names might have enslaved the human race. Perhaps a new and horrible disease marched unchecked across the land, or possibly the Earth, swept of all culture by hydrogen warfare, struggled painfully back to technological civilization while human wolfpacks roamed the badlands; or a million other equally dismal things could have happened.

And yet, Blaine thought, mankind showed an historic ability to avoid the extremes of doom as well as the extremes of bliss. Chaos was forever prophesized and utopia was continually predicted, and neither came to pass.

Accordingly, Blaine expected that this future would show certain definite improvements over the past, but he expected some deteriorations as well; some old problems would be gone, but certain others would have taken their places.

'In short,' Blaine said to himself, 'I expect that this future will be like all other futures in comparison with their pasts. That's not very specific; but then, I'm not in the predicting or the prophesying business.'

His thoughts were interrupted by Marie Thorne walking briskly into his room.

'Good morning,' she said. 'How do you feel?'

'Like a new man,' Blaine said, with a perfectly straight face.

'Good. Would you sign this, please?' She held out a pen and a typed paper.

'You're very damned efficient,' Blaine said. 'What am I signing?'

'Read it,' she said. 'It's a release absolving us from any legal responsibility in saving your life.'

'*Did* you save it?'

'Of course. How did you think you got here?'

'I didn't really think about it,' Blaine admitted.

'We saved you. But it's against the law to save lives without the potential victim's written consent. There wasn't opportunity for the Rex Corporation lawyers to obtain your consent beforehand. So we'd like to protect ourselves now.'

'What's the Rex Corporation?'

She looked annoyed. 'Hasn't anyone briefed you yet? You're inside Rex headquarters now. Our company is as well known today as Flyier-Thiess was in your time.'

'Who's Flyier-Thiess?'

'No? Ford, then?'

'Yeah, Ford. So the Rex Corporation is as well known as Ford. What does it do?'

'It manufactures Rex Power Systems,' she told him, 'which are used to power spaceships, reincarnation machines, hereafter drivers, and the like. It was an application of the Rex Power Systems that snatched you from your car at the moment after death and brought you into the future.'

'Time travel,' Blaine said. 'But how?'

'That'll be hard to explain,' she said. 'You don't have the scientific background. But I'll try. You know that space and time are the same thing, aspects of each other.'

'They are?'

'Yes. Like mass and energy. In your age, scientists knew that mass and energy were interchangeable. They were able to deduce the fission-fusion processes of the stars. But they couldn't immediately duplicate those processes, which called for vast amounts of power. It wasn't until they had the knowledge *and* the available power that they could

15

break down atoms by fission and build up new ones by fusion.'

'I know this,' Blaine said. 'What about time travel?'

'It followed the same pattern,' she said. 'For a long time we've known that space and time are aspects of the same thing. We knew that either space or time could be reduced to fundamental units and transformed into the other by a power process. We could deduce the warping of space-time in the vicinity of supernovae, and we were able to observe the disappearance of a Wolf-Rayet star when its time-conversion rate accelerated. But we had to learn a lot more. And we had to have a power source exponentially higher than you needed to set off the fusion process. When we had all this, we could interchange time units for space units – which is to say, time distances for space distances. We could then travel the distance of, say, a hundred years instead of the interchangeable distance of a hundred parsecs.'

'I see, after a fashion,' Blaine said. 'Would you mind running through it again, slowly?'

'Later, later,' she said. 'Will you please sign the release?'

The paper stated that he, Thomas Blaine, agreed not to bring suit against the Rex Corporation for their unauthorized saving of his life in the year 1958 and the subsequent transporting of that life to a Receptacle in the year 2110.

Blaine signed. 'Now,' he said, 'I'd like to know –'

He stopped. A teen-age boy had come into the room holding a large poster. 'Pardon me, Miss Thorne,' he said, 'the Art Department wants to know will this do?'

The boy held up the poster. It showed an automobile at the moment of smashup. A gigantic stylized hand was reaching down from the sky and plucking the driver from the burning wreck. The caption read: REX DID IT!

'Not bad,' Marie Thorne said, frowning judiciously. 'Tell them to brighten the reds.'

More people were coming into the room. And Blaine was growing angry.

'What's going on?' he asked.

'Later, later,' Marie Thorne said. 'Oh, Mrs. Vaness! What do you think of this poster for a teaser?'

There were a dozen people in his room now, and more coming. They clustered around Marie Thorne and the poster, ignoring Blaine completely. One man, talking earnestly to a gray-haired woman, sat down on the edge of his bed. And Blaine's temper snapped.

'Stop it!' Blaine shouted. 'I'm sick of this damned rush act. What's the matter with you people, can't you behave like human beings? Now get the hell out of here!'

'Oh Lord,' Marie Thorne sighed, closing her eyes. 'He *would* have to be temperamental. Ed, talk to him.'

A portly, perspiring middle-aged man came to Blaine's bedside. 'Mr. Blaine,' he said earnestly, 'didn't we save your life?'

'I suppose so,' Blaine said sullenly.

'We didn't have to, you know. It took a lot of time, money and trouble to save your life. But we did it. All we want in return is the publicity value.'

'Publicity value?'

'Certainly. You were saved by a Rex Power System.'

Blaine nodded, understanding now why his rebirth in the future had been accepted so casually by those around him. They had taken a lot of time, money and trouble to bring it about, had undoubtedly discussed it from every possible viewpoint, and now were conscientiously exploiting it.

'I see,' Blaine said. 'You saved me simply in order to use me as a gimmick in an advertising campaign. Is that it?'

Ed looked unhappy. 'Why put it that way? You had a life that needed saving. We had a sales campaign that needed sparking. We took care of both needs, to the mutual benefit of you and the Rex Corporation. Perhaps our motives weren't completely altruistic; would you prefer being dead?'

Blaine shook his head.

'Of course not,' Ed agreed. 'Your life is of value to you. Better alive today than dead yesterday, eh? Fine. Then why not show us a little gratitude? Why not give us a little cooperation?'

'I'd like to,' Blaine said, 'but you're moving too fast for me.'

17

'I know,' Ed said, 'and I sympathize. But you know the advertising game, Mr. Blaine. Timing is crucial. Today you're news, tomorrow nobody's interested. We have to exploit your rescue right now, while it's hot. Otherwise it's valueless to us.'

'I appreciate your saving my life,' Blaine said, 'even if it wasn't completely altruistic. I'll be glad to cooperate.'

'Thank you, Mr. Blaine,' Ed said. 'And please, no questions for a while. You'll get the picture as we go along. Miss Thorne, it's all yours.'

'Thanks, Ed,' Marie Thorne said. 'Now, everybody, we have received a provisional go-ahead from Mr. Reilly, so we'll continue as planned. Billy, you figure out a release for the morning papers. "Man from Past" sort of thing.'

'It's been done.'

'Well? It's always news, isn't it?'

'I guess once more won't hurt. So. Man from 1988 snatched –'

'Pardon me,' Blaine said. '1958.'

'So from 1958 snatched from his smashed car at the moment after death and set into a host body. Brief paragraph about the host body. Then we say that Rex Power Systems performed this snatch over one hundred and fifty-two years of time. We tell 'em how many ergs of energy we burned, or whatever it is we burn. I'll check with an engineer for the right terms. OK?'

'Mention that no other power system could have done it,' Joe said. 'Mention the new calibration system that made it possible.'

'They won't use all that.'

'They might,' Marie Thorne said. 'Now, Mrs. Vaness. We want an article on Blaine's feelings when Rex Power Systems snatched him from death. Make it emotional. Give his first sensations in the amazing world of the future. About five thousand words. We'll handle the placement.'

The gray-haired Mrs. Vaness nodded. 'Can I interview him now?'

'No time,' Miss Thorne said. 'Make it up. Thrilled, frightened, astonished, surprised at all the changes that have taken place since his time. Scientific advances. Wants to see Mars. Doesn't like the new fashions. Thinks people were happier in his own day with less gadgets and more leisure. Blaine will OK it. Won't you, Blaine?'

Blaine nodded dumbly.

'Fine. Last night we recorded his spontaneous reactions. Mike, you and the boys make that into a fifteen-minute spin which the public can buy at their local Sensory Shop. Make it a real connoisseur's item for the prestige trade. But open with a short, dignified technical explanation of how Rex made the snatch.'

'Gotcha,' said Mike.

'Right. Mr. Brice, you'll line up some solido shows for Blaine to appear on. He'll give his reactions to our age, how it feels, how it compares to his own age. See that Rex gets a mention.'

'But I don't know anything about this age!' Blaine said.

'You will,' Marie Thorne told him. 'All right, I think that's enough for a start. Let's get rolling. I'm going to show Mr. Reilly what we've planned so far.'

She turned to Blaine as the others were leaving.

'Perhaps this seems like shabby treatment. But business is business, no matter what age you're in. Tomorrow you're going to be a well-known man, and probably a wealthy one. Under the circumstances, I don't think you have any cause for complaint.'

She left. Blaine watched her go, slim and self-confident. He wondered what the penalty was, in this day and age, for striking a woman.

4

The nurse brought him lunch on a tray. The bearded doctor came in, examined him and declared him perfectly fit. There was not the slightest trace of rebirth depression, he declared, and the death trauma was obviously overrated. No reason why Blaine shouldn't be up and about.

The nurse came back with clothing, a blue shirt, brown slacks, and soft, bulbous gray shoes. The outfit, she assured him, was quite conservative.

Blaine ate with good appetite. But before dressing, he examined his new body in the full-length bathroom mirror. It was the first chance he'd had for a careful appraisal.

His former body had been tall and lean, with straight black hair and a good-humored boyish face. In thirty-two years he had grown used to that quick, deft, easy-moving body. With good grace he had accepted its constitutional flaws, its occasional illnesses, and had glorified them into virtues, into unique properties of the personality that resided within them. For his body's limitations, far more than its capabilities, seemed to express his own particular essence.

He had been fond of that body. His new body was a shock.

It was shorter than average, heavily muscled, barrel chested, broad shouldered. It felt top-heavy, for the legs were a little short in proportion to the herculean torso. His hands were large and callused. Blaine made a fist and gazed at it respectfully. He could probably fell an ox with a single blow, if an ox were procurable.

His face was square and bold, with a prominent jaw, wide cheekbones and a Roman nose. His hair was blond and curly. His eyes were a steely blue. It was a somewhat handsome, slightly brutal face.

'I don't like it,' Blaine said emphatically. 'And I hate curly blond hair.'

20

His new body had considerable physical strength; but he had always disliked sheer physical strength. The body looked clumsy, graceless, difficult to manage. It was the kind of body that bumped into chairs and stepped on people's toes, shook hands too vigorously, talked too loudly, and sweated profusely. Clothes would always bulge and constrict this body. It would need continual hard exercise. Perhaps he would even have to diet; the body looked as though it had a slight tendency toward fat.

'Physical strength is all very well,' Blaine told himself, 'if one has a purpose for it. Otherwise it's just a nuisance and a distraction, like wings on a dodo.'

The body was bad enough. But the face was worse. Blaine had never liked strong, harsh, rough-hewn faces. They were fine for sandhogs, army sergeants, jungle explorers and the like. But not for a man who enjoyed cultured society. Such a face was obviously incapable of subtlety of expression. All nuance, the delicate interplay of line and plane, would be lost. With this face you could grin or frown; only gross emotions would show.

Experimentally he smiled boyishly at the mirror. The result was a satyr's leer.

'I've been gypped,' Blaine said bitterly.

It was apparent to him that the qualities of his present mind and his new body were opposed. Cooperation between them seemed impossible. Of course, his personality might reshape his body; on the other hand, his body might have some demands to make on his personality.

'We'll see,' Blaine told his formidable body, 'we'll see who's boss.'

On his left shoulder was a long, jagged scar. He wondered how the body had received so grievous a wound. Then he began wondering where the body's real owner was. Could he still be lodged in the brain, lying doggo, waiting for a chance to take over?

Speculation was useless. Later, perhaps, he would find out. He took a final look at himself in the mirror.

He didn't like what he saw. He was afraid he never would.

21

'Well,' he said at last, 'you takes what you gets. Dead men can't be choosers.'

That was all he could say, for the moment. Blaine turned from the mirror and began dressing.

Marie Thorne came into his room late in the afternoon. She said, without preamble, 'It's off.'

'Off?'

'Finished, over, through!' She glared bitterly at him, and began pacing up and down the white room. 'The whole publicity campaign around you is off.'

Blaine stared at her. The news was interesting; but much more interesting were the signs of emotion on Miss Thorne's face. She had been so damnably controlled, so perfectly and grotesquely businesslike. Now there was color in her face, and her small lips were twisted bitterly.

'I've worked on this idea for two solid years,' she told him. 'The company's spent I don't know how many millions to bring you here. Everything's set to roll, and that damned old man says drop the whole thing.'

She's beautiful, Blaine thought, but her beauty gives her no pleasure. It's a business asset, like grooming, or a good head for liquor, to be used when necessary, and even abused. Too many hands reached to Marie Thorne, he imagined, and she never took any. And when the greedy hands kept reaching she learned contempt, then coldness, and finally self-hatred.

It's a little fanciful, Blaine thought, but I'll keep it until a better diagnosis comes along.

'That damned stupid old man,' Marie Thorne was muttering.

'What old man?'

'Reilly, our brilliant president.'

'He decided against the publicity campaign?'

'He wants it hushed up completely. Oh God, it's just too much! Two years!'

'But why?' Blaine asked.

Marie Thorne shook her head wearily. 'Two reasons, both of them stupid. First, the legal problems. I told him

22

you'd signed the release, and the lawyers had the rest of the problem in hand, but he's scared. It's almost time for his reincarnation and he doesn't want any possible legal trouble with the government. Can you imagine it? A frightened old man running Rex! Second, he had a talk with that silly, senile old grandfather of his, and his grandfather doesn't like the idea. And that clinched it. After two years!'

'Just a minute,' Blaine said. 'Did you say his *reincarnation*?'

'Yes. Reilly's going to try it. Personally I think he'd be smarter to die and get it over with.'

It was a bitter statement. But Marie Thorne didn't sound bitter making it. She sounded as though she were making a simple statement of fact.

Blaine said, 'You think he should die instead of trying for reincarnation?'

'*I* would. But I forgot, you haven't been briefed. I just wish he'd made up his mind earlier. That senile old grandfather butting in now –'

'Why didn't Reilly ask his grandfather earlier?' Blaine asked.

'He did. But his grandfather wouldn't talk earlier.'

'I see. How old is he?'

'Reilly's grandfather? He was eighty-one when he died.'

'*What?*'

'Yes, he died about sixty years ago. Reilly's father is dead, too, but he won't talk at all, which is a pity because he had good business sense. Why are you staring at me, Blaine? Oh, I forgot you don't know the setup. It's very simple, really.'

She stood for a moment, brooding. Then she nodded emphatically, whirled and walked to the door.

'Where are you going?' Blaine asked.

'To tell Reilly what I think of him! He can't do this to me! He promised!'

Abruptly her control returned.

'As for you, Blaine, I suppose there's no further need of you here. You have your life, and an adequate body in which to live it. I suppose you can leave at any time you desire.'

'Thanks,' Blaine said, as she left the room.

Dressed in his brown slacks and blue shirt, Blaine left the infirmary and walked down a long corridor until he reached a door. A uniformed guard was standing beside it.

'Excuse me,' Blaine said, 'does this door lead outside?'

'Huh?'

'Does this door lead outside the Rex Building?'

'Yeah, of course. Outside and onto the street.'

'Thank you.' Blaine hesitated. He wanted the briefing he had been promised but never given. He wanted to ask the guard what New York was like, and what the local customs and regulations were, and what he should see, and what he should avoid. But the guard apparently hadn't heard about the Man from the Past. He was staring pop-eyed at Blaine.

Blaine hated the idea of plunging into the new York of 2110 like this, without money or knowledge or friends, without a job or a place to stay, and wearing an uncomfortable new body. But it couldn't be helped. Pride meant something, after all. He would rather take his chances alone than ask assistance from the porcelain-hard Miss Thorne, or any of the others at Rex.

'Do I need a pass to get out?' he asked hopefully.

'Nope. Just to get back in.' The guard frowned suspiciously. 'Say, what's the matter with you?'

'Nothing,' Blaine said. He opened the door, still not believing that they would let him leave so casually. But then, why not? He was in a world where men talked to their dead grandfathers, where there were spaceships and hereafter drivers, where they snatched a man from the past as a publicity stunt, then lightly discarded him.

The door closed. Behind him was the great gray mass of the Rex Building. Before him lay New York.

5

At first glance, the city looked like a surrealistic Bagdad. He saw squat palaces of white and blue tile, and slender red minarets, and irregularly shaped buildings with flaring Chinese roofs and spired onion domes. It looked as though an oriental fad in architecture had swept the city. Blaine could hardly believe he was in New York. Bombay perhaps, Moscow, or even Los Angeles, but not New York. With relief he saw skyscrapers, simple and direct against the curved Asiatic structures. They seemed like lonely sentinels of the New York he had known.

The streets were filled with miniature traffic. Blaine saw motorcycles and scooters, cars no bigger than Porsches, trucks the size of Buicks, and nothing larger. He wondered if this was New York's answer to congestion and air pollution. If so, it hadn't helped.

Most of the traffic was overhead. There were vane- and jet-operated vehicles, aerial produce trucks and one-man speedsters, helicopter taxis and floating busses marked 'Skyport 2nd Level' or 'Express to Montauk.' Glittering dots marked the vertical and horizontal lanes within which the traffic glided, banked, turned, ascended and descended. Flashing red, green, yellow and blue lights seemed to regulate the flow. There were rules and conventions; but to Blaine's inexperienced eye it was a vast fluttering confusion.

Fifty feet overhead there was another shopping level. How did people get up there? For that matter, how did anyone live and retain his sanity in this noisy, bright, congested machine? The human density was overpowering. He felt as though he were being drowned in a sea of flesh. What was the population of this super-city? Fifteen million? Twenty million? It made the New York of 1958 look like a country village.

He had to stop and sort his impressions. But the sidewalks were crowded, and people pushed and cursed when he slowed down. There were no parks or benches in sight.

He noticed a group of people standing in a line, and took a place on the end. Slowly the line shuffled forward. Blaine shuffled with it, his head pounding dully, trying to catch his breath.

In a few moments he was in control of himself again, and slightly more respectful of his strong, phlegmatic body. Perhaps a man from the past needed just that sort of fleshy envelope if he wanted to view the future with equanimity. A low-order nervous system had its advantages.

The line shuffled silently forward. Blaine noticed that the men and women standing on it were poorly dressed, unkempt, unwashed. They shared a common look of sullen despair.

Was he in a breadline?

He tapped the shoulder of the man in front of him. 'Excuse me,' he said, 'where is this line going?'

The man turned his head and stared at Blaine with red-rimmed eyes. 'Going to the suicide booths,' he said, jerking his chin toward the front of the line.

Blaine thanked him and stepped quickly out of the line. What a hell of an inauspicious way to start his first real day in the future. Suicide booths! Well, he would never enter one willingly, he could be absolutely sure of that. Things surely couldn't get *that* bad.

But what kind of a world had suicide booths? And free ones, to judge by the clientele . . . He would have to be careful about accepting free gifts in this world.

Blaine walked on, gawking at the sights and slowly growing accustomed to the bright, hectic, boisterous, overcrowded city. He came to an enormous building shaped like a Gothic castle, with pennants flying from its upper battlements. On its highest tower was a brilliant green light fully visible against the fading afternoon sun.

It looked like an important landmark. Blaine stared, then noticed a man leaning against the building, lighting a thin

26

cigar. He seemed to be the only man in New York not in a tearing hurry. Blaine approached him.

'Pardon me, sir,' he said, 'what is this building?'

'This,' said the man, 'is the headquarters of Hereafter, Incorporated.' He was a tall man, very thin, with a long, mournful weatherbeaten face. His eyes were narrow and direct. His clothes hung awkwardly on him, as though he were more used to levis than tailored slacks. Blaine thought he looked like a Westerner.

'Impressive,' Blaine said, gazing up at the Gothic castle.

'Gaudy,' the man said. 'You aren't from the city, are you?'

Blaine shook his head.

'Me neither. But frankly, stranger, I thought everybody on Earth and all the planets knew about the Hereafter building. Do you mind my asking where you're from?'

'Not at all,' Blaine said. He wondered if he should proclaim himself a man from the past. No, it was hardly the thing to tell a perfect stranger. The man might call a cop. He'd better be from somewhere else.

'You see,' Blaine said, 'I'm from – Brazil.'

'Oh?'

'Yes. Upper Amazon Valley. My folks went there when I was a kid. Rubber plantation. Dad just died, so I thought I'd have a look at New York.'

'I hear it's still pretty wild down there,' the man said.

Blaine nodded, relieved that his story wasn't being questioned. But perhaps it wasn't a very strange story for this day and age. In any event, he had found a home.

'Myself,' the man said, 'I'm from Mexican Hat, Arizona. The name's Orc, Carl Orc. Blaine? Glad to meet you, Blaine. You know, I came here to cast a look around this New York and find out what they're always boasting about. It's interesting enough, but these folks are just a little too up and roaring for me, if you catch my meaning. I don't mean to say we're pokey back home. We're not. But these people bounce around like an ape with a stick in his line.'

'I know just what you mean,' Blaine said.

For a few minutes they discussed the jittery, frantic,

compulsive habits of New Yorkers, comparing them with the sane, calm, pastoral life in Mexican Hat and the Upper Amazon Valley. These people, they agreed, just didn't know how to live.

'Blaine,' said Orc, 'I'm glad I ran into you. What say we get ourselves a drink?'

'Fine,' Blaine said. Through a man like Carl Orc he might find a way out of his immediate difficulties. Perhaps he could get a job in Mexican Hat. He could plead Brazil and amnesia to excuse his lack of present-day knowledge.

Then he remembered that he had no money.

He started a halting explanation of how he had accidentally left his wallet in his hotel. But Orc stopped him in mid-sentence.

'Look here, Blaine,' Orc said, fixing him with his narrow blue eyes, 'I want to tell you something. A story like that wouldn't cut marg with most people. But I figure I'm somewhat of a judge of character. Can't say I've been wrong too often. I'm not exactly what you'd call a poor man, so what say we have the evening on me?'

'Really,' Blaine said, 'I couldn't –'

'Not another word,' Orc said decisively. 'Tomorrow evening is on you, if you insist. But right now, let us proceed to inspect the internal nocturnal movements of this edgy little old town.'

It was, Blaine decided, as good as any other way of finding out about the future. After all, nothing could be more revealing than what people did for pleasure. Through games and drunkenness, man exhibits his essential attitudes toward his environment, and shows his disposition toward the questions of life, death, fate and free will. What better symbol of Rome than the circus? What better crystallization of the American West than the rodeo? Spain had its bullfights and Norway its ski-jumps. What sport, recreation or pastime would similarly reveal the New York of 2110? He would find out. And surely, to experience this in all its immediacy was better than reading about it in some dusty library, and infinitely more entertaining.

'Suppose we have a look at the Martian Quarter?' Orc asked.

'Lead away,' Blaine said, well-pleased at the chance to combine pleasure with stern necessity.

Orc led the way through a maze of streets and levels, through underground arcades and overhead ramps, by foot, escalator, subway and helicab. The interlocking complexity of streets and levels didn't impress the lean Westerner. Phoenix was laid out in the same way, he said, although admittedly on a smaller scale.

They went to a small restaurant that called itself the 'Red Mars', and advertised a genuine South Martian cuisine. Blaine had to confess he had never eaten Martian food. Orc had sampled it several times in Phoenix.

'It's pretty good,' he told Blaine, 'but it doesn't stick to your ribs. Later we'll have a steak.'

The menu was written entirely in Martian, and no English translation was included. Blaine recklessly ordered the Number One Combination, as did Orc. It came, a strange-looking mess of shredded vegetables and bits of meat. Blaine tasted, and nearly dropped his fork in surprise.

'It's exactly like Chinese food!'

'Well, of course,' Orc said. 'The Chinese were the first on Mars, in '97 I think. So anything they eat up there is Martian food. Right?'

'I suppose so,' Blaine said.

'Besides, this stuff is made with genuine Martian-grown vegetables and mutated herbs and spices. Or so they advertise.'

Blaine didn't know whether to be disappointed or relieved. With good appetite he ate the C'kyo-Ourher, which tasted just like shrimp chow mein, and the Trrdxat, or egg roll.

'Why do they give it such weird names?' Blaine asked, ordering the Hggshrt for dessert.

'Man, you're really out of touch!' Orc said, laughing. 'Those Martian Chinese went all the way. They translated the Martian rock-carvings and suchlike, and started to talk Martian, with a strong Cantonese accent I presume, but there wasn't no one around to tell them different. They talk Martian, dress Martian, think Martian. You call one of them a Chinese now, he'd up and hit you. He's a *Martian*, boy!'

The Hggshrt came, and turned out to be an almond cookie.

Orc paid the check. As they left, Blaine asked, 'Are there many Martian laundries?'

'Hell yes. Country's filled with them.'

'I thought so,' Blaine said, and paid a silent tribute to the Martian Chinese and their firm grip on traditional institutions.

They caught a helicab to the Greens Club, a place that Orc's Phoenix friends had told him not to miss. This small, expensive, intimate little club was world-famous, an absolute must for any visitor to New York. For the Greens Club was unique in presenting an all-vegetable floor show.

They were given seats on a little balcony, not far from the glass-fenced center of the club. Three levels of tables surrounded the center, and brilliant spotlights played upon it. Behind the glass fence was what looked like a few square yards of jungle, growing in a nutrient solution. An artificial breeze stirred the plants, which were packed tight together, and varied widely in size, shape and hue.

They behaved like no plants Blaine had ever seen. They grew rapidly, fantastically, from tiny seeds and root tendrils to great shrubs and rough-barked trees, squat ferns, monstrous flowers, dripping green fungus and speckled vines; grew and quickly completed their life-cycle and fell into decay, casting forth their seeds to begin again. But no species seemed able to reproduce itself. Sports and mutants sprang from the seeds and swollen fruit, altered and adapted to the fierce environment, battled for root space below and air space above, and struggled toward the artificial suns that glowed above them. Unsuccessful shrubs quickly molded themselves into parasites, clung to the choked trees, and discovered new adaptations clinging to them in turn. Sometimes, in a burst of creative ambition, a plant would surmount all obstacles, put down the growths around it, strangle the opposition, conquer all. But new species already grew from its body, pulled it down and squabbled over the corpse. Sometimes a blight, itself vegetable, would attack the jungle and carry everything before it in a grand crescendo of mold. But a courageous sport would at last take root in it, then another, and on went the fight. The plants changed, grew larger or smaller, transcended themselves in the struggle for survival. But no amount of determination, no cunning, no transcendence helped. No species could prevail, and every endeavor led to death.

Blaine found the spectacle disturbing. Could this fatalistic pageant of the world be the significant characteristic of 2110? He glanced at Orc.

'It's really something,' Orc told him, 'what these New York labs can do with quick-growing mutants. It's a freak show, of course. They just speed up the growing rate, force a contra-survival situation, throw in some radiation, and let the best plant try to win. I hear these plants use up their growth potential in about twenty hours, and have to be replaced.'

'So that's where it ends,' Blaine said, watching the tortured but ever-optimistic jungle. 'In replacements.'

'Sure,' said Orc, blandly avoiding all philosophical complications. 'They can afford it, at the prices they charge here. But it's freak stuff. Let me tell you about the sandplants we grow in Arizona.'

Blaine sipped his whiskey and watched the jungle growing, dying and renewing itself. Orc was saying, 'Right on the burning face of the desert. Fact. We've finally adapted fruit- and vegetable-bearing plants to real desert conditions, without increasing their bulk water supply, and at a price which allows us to compete with the fertile areas. I tell you, boy, in another fifty years the entire concept of *fertile* is going to change. Take Mars, for example . . .'

They left the Greens Club and worked their way from bar to bar, toward Times Square. Orc was showing a certain difficulty in focusing, but his voice was steady as he talked about the lost Martian secret of growing on sand. Someday, he promised Blaine, we'll figure out how they produced the sandplants without the added nutrients and moisture-fixatives.

Blaine had drunk enough to put his former body into a coma twice over. But his bulky new body seemed to have an inexhaustible capacity for whiskey. It was a pleasant change, to have a body that could hold its liquor. Not, he added hastily, that such a rudimentary ability could offset the body's disadvantages.

They crossed Times Square's garish confusion and entered a bar on 44th Street. As their drinks were served, a furtive-eyed little man in a raincoat stepped up to them.

'Hey, boys,' he said tentatively.

'Whatcha want, podner?' Orc asked.

'You boys out looking for a little fun?'

'You might say so,' Orc said expansively. 'And we can find it ourselves, thank you kindly.'

The little man smiled nervously. 'You can't find what *I'm* offering.'

'Speak up, little friend,' Orc said. 'What exactly are you offering?'

'Well, boys, it's – hold it! Flathats!'

Two blue-uniformed policemen entered the bar, looked around and left.

'OK,' Blaine said. 'What is it?'

'Call me Joe,' the little man said with an ingratiating grin. 'I'm a steerer for a Transplant game, friends. The best game and highest jump in town!'

'What in hell is Transplant?' Blaine asked.

Both Orc and Joe looked at him. Joe said, 'Wow, friend, no insult but you must *really* be from down on the farm. Never heard of Transplant? Well I'll be griped!'

'OK, so I'm a farmboy,' Blaine growled, thrusting his fierce, square, hard-planed face close to Joe's. 'What is Transplant?'

'Not so loud!' Joe whispered, shrinking back. 'Take it easy, farmer, I'll explain. Transplant is the new switch game, buddy. Are you tired of living? Think you've had all

32

the kicks? Wait 'til you try Transplant. You see, farmer, folks in the know say that straight sex is pretty moldy potatoes. Don't get me wrong, it's fine for the birds and the bees and the beasts and the brutes. It still brings a thrill to their simple animal hearts, and who are we to say they're wrong? As a means of propagating the species, old nature's little sex gimmick is still the first and the best. But for real kicks, sophisticated people are turning to Transplant.

'Transplant is democratic, friends. It gives you the big chance to switch over into someone else and feel how the other ninety-nine percent feels. It's educational, you might say, and it takes up where straight sex leaves off. Ever get the urge to be a high-strung Latin, pal? You can, with Transplant. Ever wonder what a genuine sadist feels? Tune in with Transplant. And there's more, more, so much more! For example, why be a man all your life? You've proved your point by now, why belabor it? Why not be a woman for a while? With Transplant you can be aboard for those gorgeous moments in the life of one of our specially selected gals.'

'Voyeurism,' Blaine said.

'I know them big words,' Joe said, 'and it ain't true. This is no peeping-Tom's game. With Transplant *you are there*, right in the old corpus, moving those *exotic* muscles, experiencing those sensations. Ever get the urge to be a tiger, farmboy, and go loping after a lady tiger in the old mating season? We *got* a tiger, friend, and a lady tiger too. Ever ask yourself what thrill a man could possibly find in flagellation, shoe-fetichism, necrophilia, or the like? Find out with Transplant. Our catalogue of bodies reads like an encyclopedia. You can't go wrong at Transplant, friends, and our prices are set ridiculously –'

'Get out,' Blaine said.

'What, buddy?'

Blaine's big hand shot out and grabbed Joe by the raincoat front. He lifted the little pusher to eye level and glared at him.

'You take your perverted little notions out of here,' Blaine said. 'Guys like you have been selling off-beat kicks

33

since the days of Babylon, and guys like me haven't been buying. Get out, before I break your neck for a quick sadistic thrill.'

He released him. Joe smoothed his raincoat and smiled nervously. 'No offense, buddy, I'm going. Don't feel like it tonight. There's always another night. Transplant's in your future, farmboy. Why fight it?'

Blaine started to move forward, but Orc held him back. The little pusher scuttled out the door.

'He isn't worth dropping,' Orc said. 'The flathats would just take you in. It's a sad, sick, dirty world, friend. Drink up.'

Blaine threw down his whiskey, still seething. Transplant! If that was the characteristic amusement of 2110 he wanted no part of it. Orc was right, it was a sad, sick, dirty world. Even the whiskey was beginning to taste funny.

He grabbed at the bar for support. The whiskey tasted *very* funny. What was wrong with him? The stuff seemed to be going to his head.

Orc's arm was around his shoulder. He was saying, 'Well, well, my old buddy's taken himself that one too many. Guess I'd better take him back to his hotel.'

But Orc didn't know where his hotel was. He didn't even have a hotel to be taken to. Orc, that damned quick-talking straight-eyed Orc must have put something in his drink while he was talking to Joe.

In order to roll him? But Orc knew he had no money. Why then?

He tried to shake the arm off his shoulders. It was clamped in place like an iron bar. 'Don't worry,' Orc was saying, 'I'll take care of you, old buddy.'

The barroom revolved lazily around Blaine's head. He had a sudden realization that he was going to find out a great deal about 2110 by the dubious method of direct experience. Too much, he suspected. Perhaps a dusty library would have been better after all.

The barroom began to revolve more rapidly. Blaine passed out.

6

He recovered consciousness in a small, dimly lighted room with no furniture, no doors or windows, and only a single screened ventilation outlet in the ceiling. The floors and walls were thickly padded, but the padding hadn't been washed in a long time. It stank.

Blaine sat up, and two red-hot needles stabbed him through the eyes. He lay down again.

'Relax,' a voice said. 'Them knock drops take a while to wear off.'

He was not alone in the padded room. There was a man sitting in a corner, watching him. The man was wearing only shorts. Glancing at himself, Blaine saw that he was similarly dressed.

He sat up slowly and propped himself against a wall. For a moment he was afraid his head would explode. Then, as the needles drove viciously in, he was afraid it wouldn't.

'What is this?' he asked.

'End of the line,' the man said cheerfully. 'They boxed you, just like me. They boxed you and brought you in like fabrit. Now all they got to do is crate you and label you.'

Blaine couldn't understand what the man was saying. He was in no mood to decipher 2110 slang. Clutching his head, he said, 'I don't have any money. Why did they box me?'

'Come off it,' the man said. 'Why *would* they box you? They want your body, man!'

'My body?'

'Right. For a host.'

A host body, Blaine thought, such as he was now occupying. Well of course. Naturally. It was obvious when you came to think about it. This age needed a supply of host bodies for various and sundry purposes. But how do you get a host body? They don't grow on trees, nor can you dig for them. You get them from people. Most people wouldn't take kindly to selling their own bodies; life is so meaningless without one. So how to fill the supply?

Easy. You pick out a sucker, dope him, hide him away, extract his mind, then take his body.

It was an interesting line of speculation, but Blaine couldn't continue it any longer. It seemed as though his head had finally decided to explode.

Later, the hangover subsided. Blaine sat up and found a sandwich in front of him on a paper plate, and a cup of some dark beverage.

'It's safe to eat,' the man told him. 'They take good care of us. I hear the going black market price for a body is close to four thousand dollars.'

'Black market?'

'Man, what's wrong with you? Wake up! You know there's a black market in bodies just like there's an open market in bodies.'

Blaine sipped the dark beverage, which turned out to be coffee. The man introduced himself as Ray Melhill, a flow-control man off the spaceship *Bremen*. He was about Blaine's age, a compact, red-headed, snub-nosed man with slightly protruding teeth. Even in his present predicament he carried himself with a certain jaunty assurance, the unquenchable confidence of a man for whom something always turns up. His freckled skin was very white except for a small red blotch on his neck, the result of an old radiation burn.

'I should of known better,' Melhill said. 'But we'd been transiting for three months on the asteroid run and I wanted a spree. I would of been fine if I'd stuck with the boys, but we got separated. So I wound up in a dog kennel with a greasy miranda. She knocked my drink and I wound up here.'

Melhill leaned back, his hands locked behind his head. 'Me, of all people! I was always telling the boys to watch out. Stick with the gang I was always telling them. You know, I don't mind the thought of dying so much. I just hate the idea of those bastards giving my body to some dirty fat decrepit old slob so he can play around for another fifty years. That's what kills me, the thought of that fat old slob wearing my body. Christ!'

Blaine nodded somberly.

'So that's my tale of woe,' Melhill said, growing cheerful again. 'What's yours?'

'Mine's a pretty long one,' Blaine said, 'and a trifle wild in spots. Do you want to hear it all?'

'Sure. Plenty of time. I hope.'

'OK. It starts in the year 1958. Wait, don't interrupt me. I was driving my car . . .'

When he had finished, Blaine leaned back against the padded wall and took a deep breath. 'Do you believe me?' he asked.

'Why not? Nothing so new about time travel. It's just illegal and expensive. And those Rex boys would pull anything.'

'The girls, too,' Blaine said, and Melhill grinned.

They sat in companionable silence for a while. Then Blaine asked, 'So they're going to use us for host bodies?'

'That's the score.'

'When?'

'When a customer totters in. I've been here a week, close as I can figure. Either of us might be taken any second. Or it might not come for another week or two.'

'And they just wipe our minds out?'

Melhill nodded.

'But that's murder!'

'It sure is,' Melhill agreed. 'Hasn't happened yet, though. Maybe the flathats will pull a raid.'

'I doubt it.'

'Me too. Have you got hereafter insurance? Maybe you'll survive after death.'

'I'm an atheist,' Blaine said. 'I don't believe in that stuff.'

'So am I. But life after death is a fact.'

'Get off it,' Blaine said sourly.

'It is! Scientific fact!'

Blaine stared hard at the young spaceman. 'Ray,' he said,

'how about filling me in? Brief me on what's happened since 1958.'

'That's a big order,' Melhill said, 'and I'm not what you'd call an educated guy.'

'Just give me an idea. What's this hereafter stuff? And reincarnation and host bodies? What's *happening*?'

Melhill leaned back and took a deep breath. 'Well, let's see. 1958. They put a ship on the moon somewhere around 1960, and landed on Mars about ten years later. Then we had that quickie war with Russia over the asteroids – strictly a deep-space affair. Or was it with China?'

'Never mind,' Blaine said. 'What about reincarnation and life after death?'

'I'll try to give it to you like they gave it to me in high school. I had a course called Survey of Psychic Survival, but that was a long time ago. Let's see.' Melhill frowned in deep concentration. 'Quote. "Since earliest times man has sensed the presence of an invisible spirit world, and has suspected that he himself will participate in that world after the death of his body." I guess you know all about that early stuff. The Egyptians and Chinese and the European alchemists and those. So I'll skip to Rhine. He lived in your time. He was investigating psychic phenomena at Duke. Ever hear of him?'

'Sure,' Blaine said. 'What did he discover?'

'Nothing, really. But he got the ball rolling. Then Kralski took over the work at Vilna, and shoved it ahead some. That was 1987, the year the Pirates won their first World Series. Around 2000 there was Von Leddner. Outlined the general theory of the hereafter, but didn't have any proofs. And finally we come to Professor Michael Vanning.

'Professor Vanning is the boy who pinned it all down. He *proved* that people survive after death. Contacted them, talked with them, recorded them, all that stuff. Offered absolute sure-enough concrete scientific proof of life after death. So of course there were big arguments about it, a lot of religious talk. Controversy. Headlines. A big-time professor from Harvard named James Archer Flynn set out

38

to prove the whole thing was a hoax. He and Vanning argued back and forth for years.

'By this time Vanning was an old man and decided to take the plunge. He sealed a lot of stuff in a safe, hid stuff here and there, scattered some code words and promised to come back, like Houdini promised but didn't. Then –'

'Pardon me,' Blaine interrupted, 'if there *is* life after death, why didn't Houdini come back?'

'It's very simple, but please, one thing at a time. Anyhow, Vanning killed himself, leaving a long suicide note about man's immortal spirit and the indomitable progress of the human race. It's reprinted in a lot of anthologies. Later they found out it was ghost-written, but that's another story. Where was I?'

'He suicided.'

'Right. And damned if he didn't contact Professor James Archer Flynn after dying and tell him where to find all that hidden stuff, the code words, and so forth. That clinched it, buddy. Life after death was *in*.'

Melhill stood up, stretched, and sat down again. 'The Vanning Institute,' he said, 'warned everybody against hysteria. But hysteria there was. The next fifteen years are known as the Crazy Forties.'

Melhill grinned and licked his lips. 'Wish I'd been around then. Everybody just sort of let go. "Doesn't matter what you do," the jingle ran, "pie in the sky is waitin' for *you*." Saint or sinner, bad or good, everybody gets a slice. The murderer walks into the hereafter just like the archbishop. So live it up, boys and girls, enjoy the flesh on Earth while you're here, 'cause you'll get plenty of spirit after death. Yep, and they really lived it up. Anarchy it was. A new religion popped up calling itself "Realization". It started telling people that they owed it to themselves to experience *everything*, good or bad, fair and foul, because the hereafter was just a long remembrance of what you did on Earth. So *do* it, they said, that's what you're put on Earth for, *do* it, or you'll be shortchanged in the afterlife. Gratify every desire, satisfy every lust, explore your blackest depths. Live high, die high. It was wacky. The real fanatics formed torture clubs, and wrote encyclopedias on pain, and collected tortures like a housewife would collect recipes. At each meeting, a member would voluntarily present himself as a victim, and they'd kill him in the most excruciating damned ways they could find. They wanted to experience the absolute most in pleasure and pain. And I guess they did.'

Melhill wiped his forehead and said, more sedately, 'I've done a little reading on the Crazy Years.'

'So I see,' Blaine said.

'It's sort of interesting stuff. But then came the crusher. The Vanning Institute had been experimenting all this time. Around 2050, when the Crazy Years were in full swing, they announced that there was a hereafter, sure enough; *but not for everyone.*'

Blaine blinked, but made no comment.

'A real crusher. The Vanning Institute said they had certain proof that only about one person in a million got into the hereafter. The rest, the millions and millions, just went out like a light when they died. Pouf! No more. No afterlife. Nothing.'

'Why?' Blaine asked.

'Well, Tom, I'm none too clear on that part myself,' Melhill told him. 'If you asked me something about flow-mechanics, I could really tell you something; but psychic theory isn't my field. So try to stick with me while I struggle through this.'

He rubbed his forehead vigorously. 'What survives or doesn't survive after death is the mind. People have been arguing for thousands of years about what a mind is, and where and how it interacts with the body, and so forth. We haven't got all the answers, but we do have some working definitions. Nowadays, the mind is considered a high-tension energy web that emanates from the body, is modified by the body, and itself modifies the body. Got that?'

'I think so. Go on.'

'So, the way I got it, the mind and body interact and intermodify. But the mind can also exist independently of the body. According to a lot of scientists, the independent mind is the next stage of evolution. In a million years, they say, we won't even need a body except maybe for a brief incubation period. Personally I don't think this damned race will survive another million years. It damn well doesn't deserve to.'

'At the moment I agree with you,' Blaine said. 'But get back to the hereafter.'

'We've got this high-tension energy web. When the body dies, that web *should* be able to go on existing, like a butterfly coming out of a cocoon. Death is simply the process that hatches the mind from the body. But it doesn't work that way because of the death trauma. Some scientists think the death trauma is nature's ejecting mechanism, to get the mind free of the body. But it works too hard and louses up everything. Dying is a tremendous psychic shock, and most of the time the energy web gets disrupted, ripped all to hell. It can't pull itself together, it dissipates, and you're but completely dead.'

Blaine said, 'So that's why Houdini didn't come back.'

'Him and most others. Right. A lot of people did some heavy thinking, and that ended the Crazy Years. The Vanning Institute went on working. They studied Yoga and stuff like that, but on a scientific basis. Some of those Eastern religions had the right idea, you know. Strengthen the mind. That's what the institute wanted; a way to strengthen the energy web so it would survive the death process.'

'And they found it?'

'In spades. Along about that time they changed their name to Hereafter, Inc.'

Blaine nodded. 'I passed their building today. Hey, wait a minute! You say they solved the mind-strengthening problem? Then no one dies! Everyone survives after death!'

Melhill grinned sardonically. 'Don't be a farmer, Tom. You think they give it away free? Not a chance. It's a complex electrochemical treatment, pal, and they charge for it. They charge *plenty*.'

'So only the rich go to heaven,' Blaine said.

'What else did you expect? Can't have just *anyone* crashing in.'

'Sure, sure,' Blaine said. 'But aren't there other ways, other mind-strengthening disciplines? What about Yoga? What about Zen?'

'They work,' Melhill said. 'There are at least a dozen government-tested and approved home-survival courses. Trouble is, it takes about twenty years of really hard work to become an adept. That's not for the ordinary guy. Nope, without the machines to help you, you're dead.'

'And only Hereafter, Inc. has the machines?'

'There's one or two others, the Afterlife Academy and Heaven, Ltd., but the price stays about the same. The government's getting to work on some death-survival insurance, but it won't help us.'

'I guess not,' Blaine said. The dream, for a moment, had been dazzling; a relief from mortal fears; the rational certainty of a continuance and existence after the body's death; the knowledge of an uninterrupted process of growth and fulfillment for his personality to its own limits – not the constricting limits of the frail fleshy envelope that heredity and chance had imposed on him.

But that was not to be. His mind's desire to expand was to be checked, rudely, finally. Tomorrow's promises were forever not for today.

'What about reincarnation and host bodies?' he asked.

'You should know,' Melhill told him. 'They reincarnated you and put you in a host. There's nothing complicated about mind-switching, as the Transplant operators will gladly tell you. Transplant is only temporary occupancy, however, and doesn't involve full dislodgement of the original mind. Hosting is for keeps. First, the original mind must be wiped out. Second, it's a dangerous game for the mind attempting to enter the host body. Sometimes, you see, that mind can't penetrate the host and breaks itself up trying. Hereafter conditioning often won't stand up under a reincarnation attempt. If the mind doesn't make it into the host – pouf!'

Blaine nodded, now realizing why Marie Thorne had

42

thought it better for Reilly to die. Her advice had been entirely in his best interests.

He asked, 'Why would any man with hereafter insurance still make the attempt at reincarnation?'

'Because some old guys are afraid of dying,' Melhill said. 'They're afraid of the hereafter, scared of that spirit stuff. They want to stay right here on Earth where they know what's going on. So they buy a body legally on the open market, if they can find a good one. If not, they buy one on the black market. One of *our* bodies, pal.'

'The bodies on the open market are offered for sale voluntarily, then?'

Melhill nodded.

'But who would sell his body?'

'A very poor guy, obviously. By law he's supposed to receive compensation in the form of hereafter insurance for his body. In actual fact, he takes what he can get.'

'A man would have to be crazy!'

'You think so?' Melhill asked. 'Today like always, the world is filled with unskilled, sick, disease-ridden and starving people. And like always, they all got families. Suppose a guy wants to buy food for his kids? His body is the only thing of value he has to sell. Back in your time he didn't have anything to sell.'

'Perhaps so,' Blaine said. 'But no matter how bad things got, I'd never sell my body.'

Melhill laughed with good humor. 'Stout fellow! But Tom, they're taking it for nothing!'

Blaine could think of no answer for that.

7

Time passed slowly in the padded cell. Blaine and Melhill were given books and magazines. They were fed often and well, out of paper cups and plates. They were closely watched, for no harm must come to their highly marketable bodies.

They were kept together for companionship; solitary men sometimes go insane, and insanity can cause irreparable damage to the valuable brain cells. They were even granted the right to exercise, under strict supervision, to relieve boredom and to keep their bodies in shape for future owners.

Blaine began to experience an exceeding fondness for the sturdy, thickset, well-muscled body he had inhabited so recently, and from which he would be parted so soon. It was really an excellent body, he decided, a body to be proud of. True, it had no particular grace; but grace could be overrated. To counterbalance that lack, he suspected the body was not prone to hay fever like the former body he had tenanted; and its teeth were very sound.

On the whole, all considerations of mortality aside, it was not a body to be given up lightly.

One day, after they had eaten, a padded section of wall swung away. Looking in, protected by steel bars, was Carl Orc.

'Howdy,' said Orc, tall, lean, direct-eyed, angular in his city clothes, 'how's my Brazilian buddy?'

'You bastard,' Blaine said, with a deep sense of the inadequacy of words.

'Them's the breaks,' Orc said. 'You boys gettin' enough to eat?'

'You and your ranch in Arizona!'

'I've got one under lease,' Orc said. 'Mean to retire there

44

some day and raise sandplants. I reckon I know more about Arizona than many a native-born son. But ranches cost money, and hereafter insurance costs money. A man does what he can.'

'And a vulture does what *he* can,' Blaine said.

Orc sighed deeply. 'Well, it's a business, and I guess it's no worse than some others I could think of if I set my mind to it kinda hard. It's a wicked world we live in. I'll probably regret all this sometime when I'm sitting on the front porch of my little desert ranch.'

'You'll never get there,' Blaine said.

'I won't?'

'No. One night a mark is going to catch you spiking his drink. You're going to end in the gutter, Orc, with your head caved in. And that'll be the end of you.'

'Only the end of my body,' Orc corrected. 'My soul will march on to that sweet life in the by and by. I've paid my money, boy, and heaven's my next home!'

'You don't deserve it!'

Orc grinned, and even Melhill couldn't conceal a smile. Orc said, 'My poor Brazilian friend, there's no question of *deserving*. You should know better than that! Life after death just isn't for the meek and humble little people, no matter how worthy they are. It's the bright lad with the dollar in his pocket and his eyes open for number one whose soul marches on after death.'

'I can't believe it,' Blaine said. 'It isn't fair, it isn't just.'

'You're an idealist,' Orc said, interestedly, as though he were studying the world's last moa.

'Call it what you like. Maybe you'll get your hereafter, Orc. But I think there's a little corner of it where you'll burn forever!'

Orc said, 'There's no scientific evidence of hell-fire. But there's a lot we don't know about the hereafter. Maybe I'll burn. And maybe there's even a factory up there in the blue where they'll reassemble your shattered mind . . . But let's not argue. I'm sorry, I'm afraid the time's come.'

Orc walked quickly away. The steel-barred door swung open, and five men marched into the room.

45

'No!' Melhill screamed.

They closed in on the spaceman. Expertly they avoided his swinging fists and pinioned his arms. One of them pushed a gag in his mouth. They started to drag him out of the room.

Orc appeared in the doorway, frowning. 'Let go of him,' he said.

The men released Melhill.

'You idiots got the wrong man,' Orc told them. 'It's *that* one.' He pointed at Blaine.

Blaine had been trying to prepare himself for the loss of his friend. The abrupt reversal of fortune caught him open-mouthed and unready. The men seized him before he had time to react.

'Sorry,' Orc said, as they led Blaine out. 'The customer specified your particular build and complexion.'

Blaine suddenly came to life and tried to wrench free. 'I'll kill you!' he shouted to Orc. 'I swear it, I'll kill you!'

'Don't damage him,' Orc said to the men, wooden-faced.

A rag was pushed over his mouth and nose, and Blaine smelled something sickeningly sweet. Chloroform, he thought. His last recollection was of Melhill, his face ashen, standing at the barred door.

8

Thomas Blaine's first act of consciousness was to find out whether he was still Thomas Blaine, and still occupying his own body. The proof was there, apparent in the asking. They hadn't wiped out his mind yet.

He was lying on a divan, fully dressed. He sat up and heard the sound of footsteps outside, coming toward the door.

They must have overestimated the strength of the chloroform! He still had a chance!

He moved quickly behind the door. It opened, and someone walked through. Blaine stepped out and swung.

He managed to check the blow. But there was still plenty of force left when his big fist struck Marie Thorne on the side of her shapely chin.

He carried her to the divan. In a few minutes she recovered and looked at him.

'Blaine,' she said, 'you're an idiot.'

'I didn't know who it was,' Blaine said. Even as he said it, he realized it wasn't true. He *had* recognized Marie Thorne a fractional instant before the blow was irretrievably launched; and his well-machined, responsive body could have recalled the punch even then. But an unperceived, uncontrollable fury had acted beneath his sane, conscious, morally aware level; fury had cunningly used urgency to avoid responsibility; had seized the deceiving instant to smash down the cold and uncaring Miss Thorne.

The act hinted at something Blaine didn't care to know about himself. He said, 'Miss Thorne, who did you buy my body for?'

She glared at him. 'I bought it for you, since you obviously couldn't take care of it yourself.'

So he wasn't going to die after all. No fat slob was going to inherit his body, scattering his mind to the wind. Good! He

47

wanted very much to live. But he wished anyone but Marie Thorne had saved him.

'I might have done better if I'd known how things work here,' Blaine said.

'I was going to explain. Why didn't you wait?'

'After the way you talked to me?'

'I'm sorry if I was brusque,' she said. 'I was quite upset after Mr. Reilly cancelled the publicity campaign. But couldn't you understand that? If I'd been a man –'

'You aren't a man,' Blaine reminded her.

'What difference does it make? I suppose you have some strange old-fashioned ideas about woman's role and status.'

'I don't consider them strange,' Blaine said.

'Of course not.' She fingered her jaw, which was discolored and slightly swollen. 'Well, shall we consider ourselves even? Or do you want another clout at me?'

'One was enough, thank you,' Blaine said.

She stood up, somewhat unsteadily. Blaine put an arm around her to steady her, and was momentarily disconcerted. He had visualized that trim body as whipcord and steel; but in fact it was flesh, firm, resilient, and surprisingly soft. So close, he could see stray hairs escaping her tight coiffure, and a tiny mole on her forehead near the hairline. At that moment Marie Thorne ceased as an abstraction for him, and took shape as a human being.

'I can stand by myself,' she said.

After a long moment, Blaine released her.

'Under the circumstances,' she said, looking at him steadily, 'I think our relationship should remain on a strictly business level.'

Wonder after wonder! *She* had suddenly begun viewing *him* as a human being too; she was aware of him as a man, and disturbed by it. The thought gave him great pleasure. It was not, he told himself, that he liked Marie Thorne, or even desired her particularly. But he wanted very much to throw her off balance, scratch enamel off the facade, jar that damnable poise.

He said, 'Why of course, Miss Thorne.'

'I'm glad you feel that way,' she told him. 'Because frankly, you're not my type.'

'What is your type?'

'I like tall, lean men,' she said. 'Men with a certain grace, ease and sophistication.'

'But –'

'Shall we have lunch?' she said easily. 'Afterwards, Mr. Reilly would like a word with you. I believe he has a proposal to make.'

He followed her out of the room, raging inwardly. Had she been making fun of him? Tall, lean, graceful, sophisticated men! Damn it, that's what he had been! And under this beefy blond wrestler's body he still was, if only she had eyes to see it!

And who was jarring whose poise?

As they sat down at the table in the Rex executive dining room, Blaine suddenly said, 'Melhill!'

'What?'

'Ray Melhill, the man I was locked up with! Look, Miss Thorne, could you possibly buy him, too? I'll pay for it as soon as I can. We were locked up together. He's a damned nice guy.'

She looked at him curiously. 'I'll see what I can do.'

She left the table. Blaine waited, rubbing his hands together, wishing he had Carl Orc's neck between them. Marie Thorne returned in a few minutes.

'I'm very sorry,' she said. 'I contacted Orc. Mr. Melhill was sold an hour after you were removed. I really am sorry. I didn't know.'

'It's all right,' Blaine said. 'I think I'd like a drink.'

9

Mr. Reilly sat erect and almost lost in a great, soft, thronelike chair. He was a tiny, bald, spider-like old man. His wrinkled translucent skin was stretched tight across his skull and clawed hands, and bone and tendon showed clearly through the leathery, shrunken flesh. Blaine had the impression of blood coursing sluggishly through the brittle, purple varicosed veins, threatening momentarily to stop. Yet Reilly's posture was firm, and his eyes were lucid in his humorous monkey's face.

'So this is our man from the past!' Mr. Reilly said. 'Please be seated, sir. You too, Miss Thorne. I was just discussing you with my grandfather, Mr. Blaine.'

Blaine glanced around, almost expecting to see the fifty-years-dead grandfather looming spectrally over him. But there was no sign of him in the ornate, high-ceilinged room.

'He's gone now,' Mr. Reilly explained. 'Poor Grandfather can maintain an ectoplasmic state for only a brief time. But even so, he's better off than most ghosts.'

Blaine's expression must have changed, for Reilly asked, 'Don't you believe in ghosts, Mr. Blaine?'

'I'm afraid I don't.'

'Of course not. I suppose the word has unfortunate connotations for your twentieth-century mind. Clanking chains, skeletons, all that nonsense. But words change their meaning, and even reality is altered as mankind alters and manipulates nature.'

'I see,' Blaine said politely.

'You consider that doubletalk,' Mr. Reilly said good-naturedly. 'It wasn't meant to be. Consider the manner in which words change their meaning. In the twentieth century, "atoms" became a catch-all word for imaginative writers with their "atom-guns" and "atom-powered ships." An absurd word, which any level-headed man

50

would do well to ignore, just as you level-headedly ignore "ghosts." Yet a few years later, "atoms" conjured a picture of very real and imminent doom. No level-headed man could ignore the word!'

Mr. Reilly smiled reminiscently. ' "Radiation" changed from a dull textbook term to a source of cancerous ulcers. "Space-sickness" was an abstract and unloaded term in your time. But in fifty years it meant hospitals filled with twisted bodies. Words tend to change, Mr. Blaine, from an abstract, fanciful, or academic use to a functional, realistic, everyday use. It happens when manipulation catches up with theory.'

'And ghosts?'

'The process has been similar. Mr. Blaine, you're old-fashioned! You'll simply have to change your concept of the word.'

'It'll be difficult,' Blaine said.

'But necessary. Remember, there was always a lot of evidence in their favor. The prognosis for their existence, you might say, was favorable. And when life after death became fact instead of wishful thinking, ghosts became fact as well.'

'I think I'll have to see one first,' Blaine said.

'Undoubtedly you will. But enough. Tell me, how does our age suit you?'

'So far, not too well,' Blaine said.

Reilly cackled gleefully. 'Nothing endearing about body snatchers, eh? But you shouldn't have left the building, Mr. Blaine. It was not in your best interests, and certainly not in the company's best interests.'

'I'm sorry, Mr. Reilly,' Marie Thorne said. 'That was my fault.'

Reilly glanced at her, then turned back to Blaine. 'It's a pity, of course. You should, in all honesty, have been left to your destiny in 1958. Frankly, Mr. Blaine, your presence here is something of an embarrassment to us.'

'I regret that.'

'My grandfather and I agreed, belatedly I fear, against using you for publicity. The decision should have been made earlier. Still, it's made now. But there may *be* publicity, in spite of our desires. There's even a possibility of the government taking legal action against the corporation.'

'Sir,' Marie Thorne said, 'the lawyers are confident of our position.'

'Oh, we won't go to jail,' Reilly said. 'But consider the publicity. *Bad* publicity! Rex must stay respectable, Miss Thorne. Hints of scandal, innuendoes of illegality . . . No, Mr. Blaine should not be here in 2110, a walking proof of bad judgment. Therefore, sir, I'd like to make you a business proposition.'

'I'm listening,' Blaine said.

'Suppose Rex buys you hereafter insurance, thus ensuring your life after death? Would you consent to suicide?'

Blaine blinked rapidly for a moment. 'No.'

'Why not?' Reilly asked.

For a moment, the reason seemed self-evident. What creature consents to take its own life? Unhappily, man does. So Blaine had to stop and sort his thoughts.

'First of all,' he said, 'I'm not fully convinced about this hereafter.'

'Suppose we convince you,' Mr. Reilly said. 'Would you suicide then?'

'No!'

'But how shortsighted! Mr. Blaine, consider your position. This age is alien to you, inimical, unsatisfactory. What kind of work can you do? Who can you talk with, and about what? You can't even walk the streets without being in deadly peril of your life.'

'That won't happen again,' Blaine said. 'I didn't know how things worked here.'

'But it will! You can never know how things work here! Not really. You're in the same position a caveman would be, thrown haphazardly into your own 1958. He'd think himself capable enough, I suppose, on the basis of his experience with saber-tooth tigers and hairy mastodons. Perhaps some kind soul would even warn him about gangsters. But what good would it do? Would it save him from being run over by a car, electrocuted on a subway track, asphyxiated by a gas stove, falling through an elevator shaft, cut to pieces on a power saw, or breaking his neck in the bathtub? You have to be born to those things in order to walk unscathed among them. And even so, these things happened to people in your age when they relaxed their attention for a moment! How much more likely would our caveman be to stumble?'

'You're exaggerating the situation,' Blaine said, feeling a light perspiration form on his forehead.

'Am I? The dangers of the forest are as nothing to the dangers of the city. And when the city becomes a supercity –'

'I won't suicide,' Blaine said. 'I'll take my chances. Let's drop the subject.'

'Why can't you be reasonable?' Mr. Reilly asked petulantly. 'Kill yourself now and save us all a lot of trouble. I can outline your future for you if you don't. Perhaps, by sheer nerve and animal cunning, you'll survive for a year. Even two. It won't matter, in the end you'll suicide anyhow. You're a suicide type. Suicide is written all over you – you were born for it, Blaine! You'll kill yourself wretchedly in a year or two, slip out of your maimed flesh with relief – but with no hereafter to welcome your tired mind.'

'You're crazy!' Blaine cried.

'I'm never wrong about suicide types,' Mr. Reilly said quietly. 'I can always spot them. Grandfather agrees with me. So if you'll only –'

'No,' Blaine said. 'I won't kill myself. I'm afraid you'll have to hire it done.'

'That's not my way,' Mr. Reilly said. 'I won't coerce you. But come to my reincarnation this afternoon. Get a glimpse of the hereafter. Perhaps you'll change your mind.'

Blaine hesitated, and the old man grinned at him.

'No danger, I promise you, and no tricks! Did you fear I might steal your body? I selected my host months ago, from the open market. Frankly, I wouldn't *have* your body. You see, I wouldn't be comfortable in anything so gross.'

The interview was over. Marie Thorne led Blaine out.

10

The reincarnation room was arranged like a small theater. It was often used, Blaine learned, for company lectures and educational programs on an executive level. Today the audience had been kept small and select. The Rex board of directors was present, five middle-aged men sitting in the back row and talking quietly among themselves. Near them was a recording secretary. Blaine and Marie Thorne sat in front, as far from the directors as possible.

On the raised stage, under white floodlights, the reincarnation apparatus was already in place. There were two sturdy armchairs equipped with straps and wires. Between the chairs was a large glossy black machine. Thick wires connected the machine to the chair, and gave Blaine the uneasy feeling that he was going to witness an execution. Several technicians were bent over the machine, making final adjustments. Standing near them was the bearded old doctor and his red-faced colleague.

Mr. Reilly came on the stage, nodded to the audience and sat down in one of the chairs. He was followed by a man in his forties with a frightened, pale, determined face. This was the host, the present possessor of the body that Mr. Reilly had contracted for. The host sat down in the other chair, glanced quickly at the audience and looked down at his hands. He seemed embarrassed. Perspiration beaded his upper lip, and the armpits of his jacket were stained black. He didn't look at Reilly, nor did Reilly look at him.

Another man came on the stage, bald and earnest-looking, wearing a dark suit with a cleric's collar and carrying a little black book. He began a whispered conversation with the two seated men.

'Who's that?' Blaine asked.

'Father James,' Marie Thorne told him. 'He's a clergyman of the Church of the Afterlife.'

'What's that?'

'It's a new religion. You know about the Crazy Years? Well, during that time there was a great religious controversy . . .'

The burning question of the 2040's was the spiritual status of the hereafter. It became even worse after Hereafter, Inc. announced the advent of the *scientific* hereafter. The corporation tried desperately hard to avoid any religious involvement; but involvement couldn't very well be avoided. Most churchmen felt that science was unfairly pre-empting their territory. Hereafter, Inc., whether they liked it or not, was considered the spokesman for a new scientific religious position: That salvation lay, not through religious, moral or ethical considerations, but through an applied, impersonal, invariant scientific principle.

Convocations, meetings and congresses were held to decide the burning question. Some groups adopted the view that the newly revealed scientific hereafter was obviously *not* heaven, salvation, nirvana or paradise; because the soul was not involved.

Mind, they held, is not synonymous with soul; nor is the soul contained in or a part of the mind. Granted, science had found a means of extending the existence of one portion of the mind-body entity. That was fine, but it didn't affect the soul at all, and certainly didn't mean immortality or heaven or nirvana or anything like that. The *soul* could not be affected by scientific manipulation. And the soul's disposition after the eventual and inevitable death of the mind in its scientific hereafter would be in accordance with traditional moral, ethical and religious practices.

'Wow!' Blaine said. 'I think I get what you mean. They were trying to achieve a co-existence between science and religion. But wasn't their reasoning a little subtle for some people?'

'Yes,' Marie Thorne said, 'even though they explained it much better than I've done, and backed it up with all sorts of analogies. But that was only one position. Others didn't attempt co-existence. They simply declared that the scientific hereafter was sinful. And one group solved the problem by joining the scientific position and declaring that the soul *is* contained in the mind.'

'I suppose that would be the Church of the Afterlife?'

'Yes. They splintered off from other religions. According to them, the mind contains the soul, and the hereafter is the soul's rebirth after death, with no spiritual ifs and buts.'

'That's keeping up with the times,' Blaine said. 'But morality –'

'In their view, this didn't dispense with morality. The Afterlifers say that you can't impose morals and ethics on people by a system of spiritual rewards and punishments; and if you could, you shouldn't. They say that morality must be good in its own right, first in terms of the social organism, second in terms of the individual man's best good.'

To Blaine this seemed a lot to ask of morality. 'I suppose it's a popular religion?' he asked.

'Very popular,' Marie Thorne answered.

Blaine wanted to ask more, but Father James had begun speaking.

'William Fitzsimmons,' the clergyman said to the host, 'you have come to this place of your own free will, for the purpose of discontinuing your existence upon the earthly plane and resuming it upon the spiritual plane?'

'Yes, Father,' the pale host whispered.

'And the proper scientific instrumentality has been performed so that you may continue your existence upon the spiritual plane?'

'Yes, Father.'

Father James turned to Reilly. 'Kenneth Reilly, you have come to this place of your own free will for the purpose of continuing your existence upon Earth in the body of William Fitzsimmons?'

'Yes, Father,' Reilly said, small and hard-faced.

'And you have made possible for William Fitzsimmons an entrance into the hereafter; and have paid a sum of money to Fitzsimmons' heirs; and have paid the government tax involved in transactions of this kind?'

'Yes, Father,' Reilly said.

'All these things being so,' Father James said, 'no crime is involved, civic or religious. Here there is no taking of life, for the life and personality of William Fitzsimmons continues unabated in the hereafter, and the life and personality of Kenneth Reilly continues unabated upon Earth. Therefore, let the reincarnation proceed!'

To Blaine it seemed a hideous mixture of wedding ceremony and execution. The smiling clergyman withdrew. Technicians secured the men to their chairs, and attached electrodes to their arms, legs and foreheads. The theater grew very still, and the Rex directors leaned forward expectantly in their seats.

'Go ahead,' Reilly said, looking at Blaine and smiling slightly.

The chief technician turned a dial on the black machine. It hummed loudly, and the floodlights dimmed. Both men jerked convulsively against the straps, then slumped back.

Blaine whispered, 'They're murdering that poor Fitzsimmons bastard.'

'That poor bastard,' Marie Thorne told him, 'knew exactly what he was doing. He's thirty-seven years old and he's been a failure all his life. He's never been able to hold a job for long, and had no previous chance for survival after death. This was a marvellous opportunity for him. Furthermore he has a wife and five children for whom he has not been able to provide. The sum Mr. Reilly paid will enable the wife to give the children a decent education.'

'Hurray for them!' Blaine said. 'For sale, one father with slightly used body in excellent condition. Must sell! Sacrifice!'

'You're being ridiculous,' she said. 'Look, it's over.'

The machine was turned off, and the straps were removed from the two men. Reilly's wrinkled, grinning old corpse was ignored as the technicians and doctors examined the body of the host.

'Nothing yet!' the bearded old doctor called.

Blaine could sense apprehension in the room, and a hint of fear. The seconds dragged by while the doctors and technicians clustered around the host.

'Still nothing!' the old doctor called, his voice going shrill.

'What's happening?' Blaine asked Marie Thorne.

'As I told you, reincarnation is tricky and dangerous. Reilly's mind hasn't been able to possess the host-body yet. He doesn't have much longer.'

'Why not?'

'Because a body starts dying the moment it's untenanted. Irreversible death processes start if a mind isn't at least dormant in the body. The mind is essential. Even an unconscious mind controls the automatic processes. But with no mind at all –'

'Still nothing!' the old doctor shouted.

'I think it's too late now,' Marie Thorne whispered.

'A tremor!' the doctor said. 'I felt a tremor!'

There was a long silence.

'I think he's in!' the old doctor cried. 'Now, oxygen, adrenalin!'

A mask was fitted over the host's face. A hypodermic was slipped into the host's arm. The host stirred, shivered, slumped back, stirred again.

'He's made it!' the old doctor cried, removing the oxygen mask.

The directors, as though on cue, hurried out of their chairs and went up on the stage. They surrounded the host, which was now blinking its eyes and retching.

'Congratulations, Mr. Reilly!'

'Well done, sir!'

'Had us worried, Mr. Reilly!'

The host stared at them. It wiped its mouth and said, 'My name is not Reilly.'

The old doctor pushed his way through the directors and bent down beside the host. 'Not Reilly?' he said. 'Are you Fitzsimmons?'

'No,' said the host, 'I'm not Fitzsimmons, the poor damned fool! And I'm not Reilly. Reilly tried to get into this body but I was too quick. I got into the body first. It's my body now.'

'Who are you?' the doctor asked.

The host stood up. The directors stepped away from him, and one man quickly crossed himself.

'It was dead too long,' Marie Thorne said.

The host's face now bore only the faintest and most stylized resemblance to the pale, frightened face of William Fitzsimmons. There was nothing of Fitzsimmons' determination, nothing of Reilly's petulance and good humor in that face. It resembled nothing but itself.

The face was dead white except for black dots of stubble on its cheeks and jaw. The lips were bloodless. A lock of black hair was plastered against its cold white forehead. When Fitzsimmons had been in residence the features had blended pleasantly, harmoniously, nondescriptly. But now the individual features had coarsened and grown separate. The unharmonious white face had a thick and unfinished look, like iron before tempering or clay before firing. It had a slack, sullen, relaxed look because of the lack of muscle tone and tension in the face. The calm, flaccid, unharmonious features simply existed, revealing nothing of the personality behind them. The face seemed no longer completely human. All humanity now resided in the great, patient, unblinking Buddha's eyes.

'It's gone zombie,' Marie Thorne whispered, clinging to Blaine's shoulder.

'Who are you?' the old doctor asked.

'I don't remember,' it said. 'I don't.' Slowly it turned and started walking down the stage. Two directors moved tentatively to bar its path.

'Get away,' it said to them. 'It's my body now.'

'Leave the poor zombie alone,' the old doctor said wearily.

The directors moved out of its way. The zombie walked to the end of the stage, descended the steps, turned, and walked over to Blaine.

'I know you!' it said.

'What? What do you want?' Blaine asked nervously.

'I don't remember,' the zombie said, staring hard at him. 'What's your name?'

'Tom Blaine.'

The zombie shook its head. 'Doesn't mean anything to me. But I'll remember. It's you, all right. Something . . . My body's dying, isn't it? Too bad. I'll remember before it gives out. You and me, you know, together. Blaine, don't you remember me?'

'No!' Blaine shouted, shrinking from the suggested relationship, the idea of some vital link between him and this dying thing. It couldn't be! What shared secret was this thief of corpses, this unclean usurper hinting at, what black intimacy, what sniggering knowledge to be shared like a dirty crust of bread for just Blaine and himself?

Nothing, Blaine told himself. He knew himself, knew what he was, knew what he had been. Nothing like this could arise legitimately to confront him. The creature had to be crazy, or mistaken.

'Who are you?' Blaine asked.

'I don't know!' The zombie flung his hands into the air, like a man caught in a net. And Blaine sensed how his mind must feel, confused, disoriented, nameless, wanting to live and caught in the fleshy dying embrace of a zombie body.

'I'll see you again,' the zombie said to Blaine. 'You're important to me. I'll see you again and I'll remember all about you and me.'

The zombie turned and walked down the aisle and out of the theater. Blaine stared after him until he felt a sudden weight on his shoulder.

Marie Thorne had fainted. It was the most feminine thing she had done so far.

PART TWO

11

The head technician and the bearded doctor were arguing near the reincarnation machine, with their assistants ranged respectfully behind them. The battle was quite technical, but Blaine gathered that they were trying to determine the cause of the reincarnation failure. Each seemed to feel that the fault lay in the other's province.

The old doctor insisted that the machine settings must have been faulty, or an uncompensated power drop had occurred. The head technician swore the machine was perfect. He felt certain that Reilly hadn't been physically fit for the strenuous attempt.

Neither would yield an inch. But being reasonable men, they soon reached a compromise solution. The fault, they decided, lay in the nameless spirit who had fought Reilly for possession of Fitzsimmons' body, and had supplanted him.

'But who was it?' the head technician asked. 'A ghost, do you think?'

'Possibly,' the doctor said, 'though it's damned rare for a ghost to possess a living body. Still, he talked crazy enough to be a ghost.'

'Whoever he was,' the head technician said, 'he took over the host too late. The body was definitely zombie. Anyhow, no one could be blamed for it.'

'Right,' said the doctor. 'I'll certify to the apparent soundness of the equipment.'

'Fair enough,' said the head technician. 'And I'll testify to the apparent fitness of the patient.'

They exchanged a look of perfect understanding.

The directors were holding an immediate conference of their own, trying to determine what the short-range effects would be upon the Rex corporate structure, and how the announcement should be made to the public, and whether all Rex personnel should be given a day off to visit the Reilly Family Palace of Death.

Old Reilly's original body lay back in its chair, beginning to stiffen, wearing a detached, derisive grin.

Marie Thorne recovered consciousness. 'Come on,' she said, leading Blaine out of the theater. They hurried down long gray corridors to a street door. Outside, she hailed a helicab and gave the driver an address.

'Where are we going?' Blaine asked, as the helicab climbed and banked.

'To my place. Rex is going to be a madhouse for a while.' She began rearranging her hair.

Blaine settled back against the cushions and looked down on the glittering city. From that height it looked like an exquisite miniature, a multi-colored mosaic from the *Thousand and One Nights*. But somewhere down there, walking the streets and levels was the zombie, trying to remember – him.

'But why me?' Blaine asked out loud.

Marie Thorne glanced at him. 'Why you and the zombie? Well, why not? Haven't you ever made any mistakes?'

'I suppose I have. But they're finished and done with.'

She shook her head. 'Maybe mistakes ended for good in your time. Today nothing ever dies for certain. That's one of the great disadvantages of a life after death, you know. One's mistakes sometimes refuse to lie decently dead and buried. Sometimes they follow you around.'

'So I see,' Blaine said. 'But I've never done anything that would bring up *that*!'

She shrugged indifferently. 'In that case, you're better than most of us.'

Never had she seemed more alien to him. The helicab began a slow descent. And Blaine brooded over the disadvantages inherent in all advantages.

In his own time he had seen the control of disease in the world's backward areas result in an exploding birthrate, famine, plague. He had seen nuclear power breed nuclear war. Every advantage generated its own specific disadvantages. Why should it be different today?

A certified, scientific hereafter was undoubtedly an advantage to the race. Manipulation had again caught up with theory! But the disadvantages . . . There was a certain inevitable weakening of the protective barrier around mundane life, some rips in the curtain, a few holes in the dike. The dead refused to lie decently still, they insisted upon mingling with the quick. To whose advantage? Ghosts, too – undoubtedly logical, operating within the boundaries of known natural laws. But that might be cold comfort to a haunted man.

Today, Blaine thought, a whole new stratum of existence impinged upon man's existence on Earth. Just as the zombie impinged uncomfortably on *his* existence.

The helicab landed on the roof of an apartment building. Marie Thorne paid, and led Blaine to her apartment.

It was a large airy apartment, pleasingly feminine, and furnished with a certain dramatic flair. There was more bright color than Blaine would have thought compatible with Miss Thorne's sombre personality; but perhaps the vivid yellows and sharp reds expressed a wish of some sort, a compensation for the restraint of her business life. Or perhaps it was just the prevailing style. The apartment contained the sort of gadgetry that Blaine associated with the future; self-adjusting lighting and air-conditioning, self-conforming armchairs, and a push-button bar that produced an adequate Martini.

Marie Thorne went into one of the bedrooms. She returned in a high-collared housedress and sat down on a couch opposite him.

'Well, Blaine, what are your plans?'

'I thought I'd ask you for a loan.'

'Certainly.'

'In that case my plan is to find a hotel room and start looking for a job.'

'It won't be easy,' she said, 'but I know some people who might –'

'No thanks,' Blaine said. 'I hope this doesn't sound too silly, but I'd rather find a job on my own.'

'No, it doesn't sound silly. I just hope it's possible. How about some dinner?'

'Fine. Do you cook, too?'

'I set dials,' she told him. 'Let's see. How would you like a genuine Martian meal?'

'No thanks,' Blaine said. 'Martian food is tasty, but it doesn't stick to your ribs. Would you happen to have a steak around the place?'

Marie set the dials and her auto-chef did the rest, selecting the food from pantry and freezer, peeling, unwrapping, washing and cooking them, and ordering new items to replace those used. The meal was perfect; but Marie seemed oddly embarrassed about it. She apologized to Blaine for the completely mechanical operation. After all, he came from an age in which women had opened their own cans, and done their own tasting; but they'd probably had more leisure time, too.

The sun had set by the time they finished their coffee. Blaine said, 'Thank you very much, Miss Thorne. Now if you could loan me that money, I'll get started.'

She looked surprised. 'At night?'

'I'll find a hotel room. You've been very kind, but I wouldn't want to presume any further –'

'That's all right,' she said. 'Stay here tonight.'

'All right,' Blaine said. His mouth was suddenly dry, and his heart was pounding with suspicious rapidity. He knew there was nothing personal in her invitation; but his body didn't seem to understand. It insisted upon reacting hopefully, expectantly even, to the controlled and anti-septic Miss Thorne.

She gave him a bedroom and a pair of green pajamas. Blaine closed the door when she left, undressed and got into bed. The light went out when he told it to.

In a little while, just as his body had expected, Miss Thorne came in wearing something white and gossamer, and lay down beside him.

They lay side by side in silence. Marie Thorne moved closer to him, and Blaine slipped an arm under her head.

He said, 'I thought you weren't attracted to my type.'

'Not exactly. I said I *preferred* tall, lean men.'

'I was once a tall, lean man.'

'I suspected it,' she said.

They were both silent. Blaine began to grow uncomfortable and apprehensive. What did this mean? Had she some fondness for him? Or was this simply a custom of the age, a sort of Eskimo hospitality?

'Miss Thorne,' he said, 'I wonder if –'

'Oh be quiet!' she said, suddenly turning toward him, her eyes enormous in the shadowy room. 'Do you have to question everything, Tom?'

Later she said, dreamily, 'Under the circumstances, I think you can call me Marie.'

In the morning Blaine showered, shaved and dressed. Marie dialed a breakfast for them. After they had eaten she gave him a small envelope.

'I can loan you more when you need it,' she said. 'Now about finding a job –'

'You've helped me very much,' Blaine said. 'The rest I'd like to do on my own.'

'All right. My address and telephone number are on the envelope. Please call me as soon as you have a hotel.'

'I will,' Blaine said, watching her closely. There was no hint of the Marie of last night. It might have been a different person entirely. But her studied self-possession was reaction enough for Blaine. Enough, at least for the moment.

At the door she touched his arm. 'Tom,' she said, 'please be careful. And call me.'

'I will, Marie,' Blaine said.

He went into the city happy and refreshed, and intent upon conquering the world.

12

Blaine's first idea had been to make a round of the yacht-design offices. But he decided against it simply by picturing a yacht designer from 1806 walking into an office in 1958.

The quaint old man might be very talented; but how would that help him when he was asked what he knew about metacentric shelf analysis, flow diagrams, centers of effort, and the best locations for RDF and sonar? What company would pay him while he learned the facts about reduction gears, exfoliating paints, tank testing, propeller pitch, heat exchange systems, synthetic sailcloth . . . ?

Not a chance, Blaine decided. He couldn't walk into a design office 152 years behind the times and ask for a job. A job as *what*? Perhaps he could study and catch up to 2110 technology. But he'd have to do it on his own time.

Right now, he'd take anything he could get.

He went to a newsstand and purchased a microfilm *New York Times* and a viewer. He walked until he found a bench, sat down and turned to the classified ads. Quickly he skipped past the skilled categories, where he couldn't hope to qualify, and came to unskilled labor. He read:

'Set-up man wanted in auto-cafeteria. Requires only basic knowledge of robotics.'

'Hull wiper wanted, Mar-Coling liner. Must be Rh positive and fortified anticlaustrophobiac.'

'List man needed for hi-tensile bearing decay work. Needs simple jenkling knowledge. Meals included.'

It was apparent to Blaine that even the unskilled labor of 2110 was beyond his present capacity. Turning the page to Employment for Boys, he read:

'Wanted, young man interested in slic-trug machinery. Good future. Must know basic calculus and have working knowledge Hootean Equations.'

'Young Men wanted, salesmen's jobs on Venus. Salary

plus commission. Knowledge basic French, German, Russian and Ourescz.'

'Delivery, Magazine, Newspaper boys wanted by Eth-Col agency. Must be able to drive a Sprening. Good knowledge of city required.'

So – he couldn't even qualify as a newsboy!

It was a depressing thought. Finding a job was going to be more difficult than he had imagined. Didn't anyone dig ditches or carry packages in this city? Did robots do all the menial work, or did you need a Ph.D. even to lug a wheelbarrow? What sort of world was this?

He turned to the front page of the *Times* for an answer, adjusted his viewer, and read the news of the day:

A new spacefield was under construction at Oxa, New South Mars.

A poltergeist was believed responsible for several industrial fires in the Chicago area. Tentative exorcism proceedings were under way.

Rich copper deposits had been discovered in the Sigma-G sector of the asteroid belt.

Doppelganger activities had increased in Berlin.

A new survey was being made of octopi villages in the Mindanao Deep.

A mob in Spenser, Alabama, lynched and burned the town's two local zombies. Legal action was being taken against the mob leaders.

A leading anthropologist declared the Tuamoto Archipelago in Oceania to be the last stronghold of 20th century simplicity.

The Atlantic Fish Herders' Association was holding its annual convention at the Waldorf.

A werewolf was unsuccessfully hunted in the Austrian Tyrol. Local villages were warned to keep a twenty-four-hour watch for the beast.

A bill was introduced into the House of Representatives to outlaw all hunts and gladiatorial events. It was defeated.

A berserker took four lives in downtown San Diego.

Helicopter fatalities reached the one million mark for the year.

Blaine put the newpaper aside, more depressed than ever. Ghosts, doppelgangers, werewolves, poltergeists . . . He didn't like the sound of those vague, grim, ancient words which today seemed to represent actual phenomena. He had already met a zombie. He didn't want to encounter any more of the dangerous side-effects of the hereafter.

He started walking again. He went through the theater district, past glittering marquees, posters advertising the gladiatorial events at Madison Square Garden, billboards heralding solidovision programs and sensory shows, flashing signs proclaiming overtone concerts and Venusian pantomime. Sadly Blaine remembered that *he* might have been part of this dazzling fairyland if only Reilly hadn't changed his mind. He might be appearing at one of those theaters now, billed as the Man from the Past . . .

Of course! A Man from the Past, Blaine suddenly realized, had a unique and indisputable novelty value, an inherent talent. The Rex Corporation had saved his life in 1958 solely in order to use that talent. But they had changed their minds. So what was to prevent him from using his novelty value for himself? And for that matter, what else could he do? Show business looked like the only possible business for him.

He hurried into a gigantic office building and found six theatrical agents listed on the board. He picked Barnex, Scofield & Styles, and took the elevator to their offices on the 19th floor.

He entered a luxurious waiting room panelled with gigantic solidographs of smiling actresses. At the far end of the room, a pretty receptionist raised an inquiring eyebrow at him.

Blaine went up to her desk. 'I'd like to see someone about my act,' he told her.

'I'm so sorry,' she said. 'We're all filled.'

'This is a very special act.'

'I'm really terribly sorry. Perhaps next week.'

'Look,' Blaine said, 'my act is really unique. You see, I'm a man from the past.'

'I don't care if you're the ghost of Scott Merrivale,' she said sweetly. 'We're *filled*. Try us next week.'

70

Blaine turned to go. A short, stocky man breezed past him, nodding to the receptionist.

'Morning, Miss Thatcher.'

'Morning, Mr. Barnex.'

Barnex! One of the agents! Blaine hurried after him and grabbed his sleeve.

'Mr. Barnex,' he said, 'I have an act –'

'Everybody has an act,' Barnex said wearily.

'But this act is unique!'

'Everybody's act is unique,' Barnex said. 'Let go my sleeve, friend. Try us next week.'

'I'm from the past!' Blaine cried, suddenly feeling foolish. Barnex turned and stared at him. He looked as though he might be on the verge of calling the police, or Bellevue. But Blaine plunged recklessly on.

'I really am!' he said. 'I have absolute proof. The Rex Corporation snatched me out of the past. Ask them!'

'Rex?' Barnex said. 'Yeah, I heard something about that snatch over at Lindy's . . . Hmm. Come into my office, Mister –'

'Blaine, Tom Blaine.' He followed Barnex into a tiny, cluttered cubicle. 'Do you think you can use me?' he asked.

'Maybe,' Barnex said, motioning Blaine to a chair. 'It depends. Tell me, Mr. Blaine, what period of the past are you from?'

'In 1958. I have an intimate knowledge of the nineteen thirties, forties and fifties. By way of stage experience I did some acting in college, and a professional actress friend of mine once told me I had a natural way of –'

'1958? That's 20th Century?'

'Yes, that's right.'

The agent shook his head. 'Too bad. Now if you'd been a 6th Century Swede or a 7th Century Jap, I could have found work for you. I've had no difficulty booking appearances for our 1st Century Roman or our 4th Century Saxon, and I could use a couple more like them. But it's damned hard finding anyone from those early centuries, now that time travel is illegal. And B.C. is completely out.'

'But what about the 20th Century?' Blaine asked.

'It's filled.'

'Filled?'

'Sure. Ben Therler from 1953 gets all the available stage appearances.'

'I see,' Blaine said, getting slowly to his feet. 'Thanks anyhow, Mr. Barnex.'

'Not at all,' Barnex said. 'Wish I could help. If you'd been from any time or place before the 11th Century, I could probably book you. But there's not much interest in recent stuff like the 19th and 20th Centuries . . . Say, why don't you go see Therler? It isn't likely, but maybe he can use an understudy or something.' He scrawled an address on a piece of paper and handed it to Blaine.

Blaine took it, thanked him again, and left.

In the street he stood for a moment, cursing his luck. His one unique and indisputable talent, his novelty value, had been usurped by Ben Therler of 1953! Really, he thought, time travel should be kept more exclusive. It just wasn't fair to drop a man here and then ignore him.

He wondered what sort of man Therler was. Well, he'd find out. Even if Therler didn't need an understudy, it would be a pleasure and relief to talk to someone from home. And Therler, who had lived here longer, might have some ideas on what a 20th century man could do in 2110.

He flagged a helicab and gave him the address. In fifteen minutes he was in Therler's apartment building, pressing the doorbell.

The door was opened by a sleek, chubby, complacent-looking man wearing a dressing gown.

'You the photographer?' he asked. 'You're too early.'

Blaine shook his head. 'Mr. Therler, you've never met me before. I'm from your own century. I'm from 1958.'

'Is that so?' Therler asked, with obvious suspicion.

'It's the truth,' Blaine said. 'I was snatched by the Rex Corporation. You can check my story with them.'

Therler shrugged his shoulders. 'Well, what is it you want?'

72

'I was hoping you might be able to use an understudy or something –'

'No, no, I never use an understudy,' Therler said, starting to close the door.

'I didn't think so,' Blaine said. 'The real reason I came was just to talk to you. It gets pretty lonely being out of one's century. I wanted to talk to someone from my own age. I thought maybe you'd feel that way, too.'

'Me? Oh!' Therler said, smiling with sudden stage warmth. 'Oh, you mean about the good old twentieth century! I'd love to talk to you about it sometime, pal. Little old New York! The Dodgers and Yankees, the hansoms in the park, the roller-skating rink in Rockefeller Plaza. I sure miss it all! Boy! But I'm afraid I'm a little busy now.'

'Certainly,' Blaine said. 'Some other time.'

'Fine! I'd really love to!' Therler said, smiling even more brilliantly. 'Call my secretary, will you, old man? Schedules, you know. We'll have a really great old gab some one of these days. I suppose you could use a spare dollar or two –'

Blaine shook his head.

'Then, 'bye,' Therler said heartily. 'And do call soon.'

Blaine hurried out of the building. It was bad enough being robbed of your novelty value; it was worse being robbed by an out-and-out phony, a temporal fraud who'd never been within a hundred years of 1953. The Rockefeller *roller*-skating rink! And even that slip hadn't been necessary. Everything about the man screamed counterfeit.

But sadly, Blaine was probably the only man in 2110 who could detect the imposture.

That afternoon Blaine purchased a change of clothing and a shaving kit. He found a room in a cheap hotel on Fifth Avenue. For the next week, he continued looking for work.

He tried the restaurants, but found that human dish-washers were a thing of the past. At the docks and spaceports, robots were doing most of the heavy work. One day he was tentatively approved for a position as package-wrapping inspector at Gimbel-Macy's. But the personnel department, after carefully studying his personality profile, irritability index and suggestibility rating, vetoed him in favor of a dull-eyed little man from Queens who held a master's degree in package design.

Blaine was wearily returning to his hotel one evening when he recognized a face in the dense crowd. It was a man he would have known instantly, anywhere. He was about Blaine's age, a compact, red-headed, snub-nosed man with slightly protruding teeth and a small red blotch on his neck. He carried himself with a certain jaunty assurance, the unquenchable confidence of a man for whom something always turns up.

'Ray!' Blaine shouted. 'Ray Melhill!' He pushed through the crowd and seized him by the arm. 'Ray! How'd you get out?'

The man pulled his arm away and smoothed the sleeve of his jacket. 'My name is not Melhill,' he said.

'It's not? Are you sure?'

'Of course I'm sure,' he said, starting to move away.

Blaine stepped in front of him. 'Wait a minute. You look exactly like him, even down to the radiation scar. Are you *sure* you aren't Ray Melhill, a flow-control man off the spaceship *Bremen*?'

'Quite certain,' the man said coldly. 'You have confused me with someone else, young man.'

Blaine stared hard as the man started to walk away. Then he reached out, caught the man by a shoulder and swung him around.

'You dirty body-thieving bastard!' Blaine shouted, his big right fist shooting out.

The man who so exactly resembled Melhill was knocked back against a building, and slid groggily to the pavement. Blaine started for him, and people moved quickly out of his way.

'Berserker!' a woman screamed, and someone else took up the cry. Blaine caught sight of a blue uniform shoving through the crowd toward him.

A flathat! Blaine ducked into the crowd. He turned a corner quickly, then another, slowed to a walk and looked

74

back. The policeman was not in sight. Blaine started walking again to his hotel.

It had been Melhill's body; but Ray no longer occupied it. There had been no last-minute reprieve for him, no final chance. His body had been taken from him and sold to the old man whose querulous mind wore the jaunty body like a suit of ill-fitting, too-youthful clothes.

Now he knew his friend was really dead. Blaine drank silently to him in a neighborhood bar before returning to his hotel.

The clerk stopped him as he passed the desk. 'Blaine? Got a message for you. Just a minute.' He went into the office.

Blaine waited, wondering who it could be from. Marie? But he hadn't called Marie yet, and wasn't planning to until he found work.

The clerk came back and handed him a slip of paper. The message read: 'There is a Communication awaiting Thomas Blaine at the Spiritual Switchboard, 23rd Street Branch. Hours, nine to five.'

'I wonder how anybody knew where I was?' Blaine asked.

'Spirits got their ways,' the clerk told him. 'Man I know, his dead mother-in-law tracked him down through three aliases, a Transplant and a complete skin job. He was hiding from her in Abyssinia.'

'I don't have any dead mother-in-law,' Blaine said.

'No? Who you figure's trying to reach you?' the clerk asked.

'I'll find out tomorrow and let you know,' Blaine said. But his sarcasm was wasted. The clerk had already turned back to his correspondence course on Atomic Engine Maintenance. Blaine went up to his room.

13

The 23rd Street Branch of the Spiritual Switchboard was a large greystone building near Third Avenue. Engraved above the door was the statement: 'Dedicated to Free Communication Between Those on Earth and Those Beyond.'

Blaine entered the building and studied the directory. It gave floor and room numbers for Messages Incoming, Messages Outgoing, Translations, Abjurations, Exorcisms, Offerings, Pleas, and Exhortations. He wasn't sure which classification he fell under, or what the classifications signified, or even the purpose of the Spiritual Switchboard. He took his slip of paper to the information booth.

'That's Messages Incoming,' a pleasant, gray-haired receptionist told him. 'Straight down the hall to room 32A.'

'Thank you.' Blaine hesitated, then said, 'Could you explain something to me?'

'Certainly,' the woman said. 'What do you wish to know?'

'Well – I hope this doesn't sound too foolish – what *is* all this?'

The gray-haired woman smiled. 'That's a difficult question to answer. In a philosophical sense I suppose you might call the Spiritual Switchboard a move toward greater oneness, an attempt to discard the dualism of mind and body and substitute –'

'No,' Blaine said. 'I mean literally.'

'Literally? Why, the Spiritual Switchboard is a privately endowed, tax-free organization, chartered to act as a clearing house and center for communications to and from the Threshold plane of the Hereafter. In some cases, of course, people don't need our aid and can communicate directly with their departed ones. But more often, there is a need for amplification. This center possesses the proper

76

equipment to make the deceased audible to our ears. And we perform other services, such as abjurations, exorcisms, exhortations and the like, which become necessary from time to time when flesh interacts with spirit.'

She smiled warmly at him. 'Does that make it any clearer?'

'Thank you very much,' Blaine said, and went down the hall to room 32A.

It was a small gray room with several armchairs and a loudspeaker set in the wall. Blaine sat down, wondering what was going to happen.

'Tom Blaine!' cried a disembodied voice from the loudspeaker.

'Huh? What?' Blaine asked, jumping to his feet and moving toward the door.

'Tom! How are you, boy?'

Blaine, his hand on the doorknob, suddenly recognized the voice. 'Ray Melhill?'

'Right! I'm up there where the rich folks go when they die! Pretty good, huh?'

'That's the understatement of the age,' Blaine said. 'But Ray, *how*? I thought you didn't have any hereafter insurance.'

'I didn't. Let me tell you the whole story. They came for me maybe an hour after they took you. I was so damned angry I thought I'd go out of my mind. I stayed angry right through the chloroforming, right through the wiping. I was still angry when I died.'

'What was dying like?' Blaine asked.

'It was like exploding. I could feel myself scattering all over the place, growing big as the galaxy, bursting into fragments, and the fragments bursting into smaller fragments, and all of them were *me*.'

'And what happened?'

'I don't know. Maybe being so angry helped. I was stretched as far as I could go – any further and it wouldn't be me – and then I just simply came back together again. Some people do. Like I told you, a few out of every million have always survived without hereafter training. I was one of the lucky ones.'

'I guess you know about me,' Blaine said. 'I tried to do something for you, but you'd already been sold.'

'I know,' Melhill said. 'Thanks anyhow, Tom. And say, thanks for popping that slob. The one wearing my body.'

'You saw that?'

'I been keeping my eyes open,' Melhill said. 'By the way, I like that Marie. Nice-looking kid.'

'Thanks. Ray, what's the hereafter like?'

'I don't know.'

'You don't?'

'I'm not *in* the hereafter yet, Tom. I'm in the Threshold. It's a preparatory stage, a sort of bridge between Earth and the hereafter. It's hard to describe. A sort of grayness, with Earth on one side and the hereafter on the other.'

'Why don't you cross over?' Blaine asked.

'Not yet,' Melhill said. 'It's a one-way street into the hereafter. Once you cross over, you can't come back. There's no more contact with Earth.'

Blaine thought about that for a moment, then asked, 'When are you going to cross over, Ray?'

'I don't rightly know. I thought I'd stay in Threshold for a while and keep an eye on things.'

'Keep an eye on me, you mean.'

'Well . . .'

'Thanks a lot, Ray, but don't do it. Go into the hereafter. I can take care of myself.'

'Sure you can,' Melhill said. 'But I think I'll stick around for a while anyhow. You'd do it for me, wouldn't you? So don't argue. Now look, I suppose you know you're in trouble?'

Blaine nodded. 'You mean the zombie?'

'I don't know who he is or what he wants from you, Tom, but it can't be good. You'd better be a long way off when he finds out. But that wasn't the trouble I meant.'

'You mean I have more?'

'Afraid so. You're going to be haunted, Tom.'

In spite of himself, Blaine laughed.

'What's so funny?' Melhill asked indignantly. 'You think it's a *joke* to be haunted?'

'I suppose not. But is it really so serious?'

'Lord, you're ignorant,' Melhill said. 'Do you know anything about ghosts? How they're made and what they want?'

'Tell me.'

'Well, there are three possibilities when a man dies. First, his mind can just explode, scatter, dissipate; and that's the end of him. Second, his mind can hold together through the death trauma; and he finds himself in the Threshold, a spirit. I guess you know about those two.'

'Go on,' Blaine said.

'The third possibility is this: His mind breaks during the death trauma, but not enough to cause dissipation. He pulls through into the Threshold. But the strain has been permanently disabling. He's insane. And that, my friend, is how a ghost is born.'

'Hmm,' Blaine said. 'So a ghost is a mind that went insane during the death trauma?'

'Right. He's insane, and he haunts.'

'But why?'

'Ghosts haunt,' Melhill said, 'because they're filled with twisted hatred, anger, fear and pain. They won't go into the hereafter. They want to spend as much time as they can on Earth, where their attention is still fixed. They want to frighten people, hurt them, drive them insane. Haunting is the most asocial thing they can do, it's their madness. Look Tom, since the beginning of mankind . . .'

Since the beginning of mankind there have been ghosts, but their numbers have always been small. Only a few out of every million people managed to survive after death; and only a tiny percentage of those survivors went insane during the transition, and became ghosts.

But the impact of those few was colossal upon a mankind fascinated by death, awed by the cold uncaring mobility of the corpse so recently quick and vital, shocked at the ghastly inapropos humor of the skeleton. Death's elaborate, mysterious figure seemed infinitely meaningful, its warning finger pointed toward the spirit-laden skies. So for every genuine ghost, rumor and fear produced a thousand. Every gibbering bat became a ghost. Marsh-fires, flapping curtains and swaying trees became ghosts, and St. Elmo's fire, great-eyed owls, rats in the walls, foxes in the bush, all became ghostly evidence. Folklore grew and produced witch and warlock, evil little familiars, demons and devils, succubi and incubi, werewolf and vampire. For every ghost a thousand were suspected, and for every supernatural fact a million were assumed.

Early scientific investigators entered this maze, trying to discover the truth about supernatural phenomena. They uncovered countless frauds, hallucinations and errors of judgment. And they found a few genuinely inexplicable events, which, though interesting, were statistically insignificant.

The whole tradition of folklore came tumbling down. Statistically there were no ghosts. But continually there was a sly, elusive *something* which refused to stand still and be classified. It was ignored for centuries, the occasional *something* which gave a basis and reality to tales of incubi and succubi. Until at last scientific theory caught up with folklore, made a place for it in the realm of indisputable phenomena, and gave it respectability.

With the discovery of the scientific hereafter, the irrational ghost became understandable as a demented mind inhabiting the misty interface between Earth and the hereafter. The forms of ghostly madness could be categorized like madness on Earth. There were the melancholics, drifting disconsolately through the scenes of their great passion; the whispering hebephrenic, chattering gay and random nonsense; the idiots and imbeciles who returned in the guise of little children; the schizophrenics who imagined themselves to be animals, prototypes of vampire and Abominable Snowman, werewolf, weretiger, werefox, weredog. There were the destructive stone-throwing and fire-setting ghosts, the poltergeists, and the grandiloquent paranoids who imagined themselves to be Lucifer or Beelzebub, Israfael or Azazael, the Spirit of Christmas Past, the Furies, Divine Justice, or even Death itself.

Haunting was madness. They wept by the old watch tower, these few ghosts upon whose gossamer shoulders rested the entire great structure of folklore, mingled with the mists around the gibbet, jabbered their nonsense at the seance. They talked, cried, danced and sang for the delectation of the credulous, until scientific observers came with their sober cold questions. Then they fled back to the Threshold, terrified of this onslaught of reason, protective of their delusions, fearful of being cured.

'So that's how it was,' Melhill said. 'You can figure out the rest. Since Hereafter, Inc. a hell of a lot more people are surviving after death. But of course a lot more are going insane on the way.'

'Thus producing a lot more ghosts,' Blaine said.

'Right. One of them is after you,' Melhill said, his voice growing faint. 'So watch your step. Tom, I gotta go now.'

'What kind of ghost is it?' Blaine asked. 'Whose ghost? And why do you have to go?'

'It takes energy to stay on Earth,' Melhill whispered. 'I'm just about used up. Have to recharge. Can you still hear me?'

'Yes, go on.'

'I don't know when the ghost will show himself, Tom. And I don't know who he is. I asked, but he wouldn't tell me. Just watch out for him.'

'I'll watch out,' Blaine said, his ear pressed to the loudspeaker. 'Ray! Will I speak to you again?'

'I think so,' Melhill said, his voice barely audible. 'Tom, I know you're looking for a job. Try Ed Franchel, 322 West 19th Street. It's rough stuff, but it pays. And watch yourself.'

'Ray!' Blaine shouted. 'What *kind* of a ghost is it?'

There was no answer. The loudspeaker was silent, and he was alone in the gray room.

14

322 West 19th Street, the address Ray Melhill had given him, was a small, dilapidated brownstone near the docks. Blaine climbed the steps and pressed the ground-floor buzzer marked *Edward J. Franchel Enterprises*. The door was opened by a large, balding man in shirtsleeves.

'Mr. Franchel?' Blaine asked.

'That's me,' the balding man said, with a resolutely cheerful smile. 'Right this way, sir.'

He led Blaine into an apartment pungent with the odor of boiled cabbage. The front half of the apartment was arranged as an office, with a paper-cluttered desk, a dusty filing cabinet and several stiff-backed chairs. Past it, Blaine could see a gloomy living room. From the inner recesses of the apartment a solido was blaring out a daytime show.

'Please excuse the appearance,' Franchel said, motioning Blaine to a chair. 'I'm moving into a regular office uptown just as soon as I find time. The orders have been coming in so fast and furious . . . Now sir, what can I do for you?'

'I'm looking for a job,' Blaine said.

'Hell,' said Franchel, 'I thought you were a customer.' He turned in the direction of the blaring solido and shouted, 'Alice, will you turn that goddamned thing down?' He waited until the volume had receded somewhat, then turned back to Blaine. 'Brother, if business doesn't pick up soon I'm going back to running a suicide booth at Coney. A job, huh?'

'That's right. Ray Melhill told me to try you.'

Franchel's expression brightened. 'How's Ray doing?'

'He's dead.'

'Shame,' Franchel said. 'He was a good lad, though always a bit wild. He worked for me a couple of times when the space pilots were on strike. Want a drink?'

Blaine nodded. Franchel went to the filing cabinet and

removed a bottle of rye whiskey labelled 'Moonjuice.' He found two shot glasses and filled them with a practiced flourish.

'Here's to old Ray,' Franchel said. 'I suppose he got himself boxed?'

'Boxed and crated,' Blaine said. 'I just spoke to him at the Spiritual Switchboard.'

'Then he made Threshold!' Franchel said admiringly. 'Friend, *we* should only have his luck. So you want a job? Well, maybe I can fix it. Stand up.'

He walked around Blaine, touched his biceps and ran a hand over his ridged shoulder muscles. He stood in front of Blaine, nodding to himself with downcast eyes, then feinted a quick blow at his face. Blaine's right hand came up instantly, in time to block the punch.

'Good build, good reflexes,' Franchel said. 'I think you'll do. Know anything about weapons?'

'Not much,' Blaine said, wondering what kind of job he was getting into. 'Just – ah – antiques. Garands, Winchesters, Colts.'

'No kidding?' Franchel said. 'You know, I always wanted to collect antique recoil arms. But no projectile or beam weapons are allowed on this hunt. What else you got?'

'I can handle a rifle with bayonet,' Blaine said, thinking how his basic-training sergeant would have roared at that overstatement.

'You can? Lunges and parries and all? Well I'll be damned, I thought bayonetry was a lost art. You're the first I've seen in fifteen years. Friend, you're hired.'

Franchel went to his desk, scribbled on a piece of paper and handed it to Blaine.

'You go to that address tomorrow for your briefing. You'll be paid standard hunter's salary, two hundred dollars plus fifty a day for every working day. Have you got your own weapons and equipment? Well, I'll pick the stuff up for you, but it's deducted from your pay. And I take ten percent off the top. OK?'

'Sure,' Blaine said. 'Could you explain a little more about the hunt?'

'Nothing to explain. It's just a standard hunt. But don't go around talking about it. I'm not sure if hunts are still legal. I wish Congress would straighten out the Suicide and Permitted Murder Acts once and for all. A man doesn't know where he's at any more.'

'Yeah,' Blaine agreed.

'They'll probably discuss the legal aspects at the briefing,' Franchel said. 'The hunters will be there, and the Quarry will tell you all you need to know. Say hello to Ray for me if you speak to him again. Tell him I'm sorry he got killed.'

'I'll tell him,' Blaine said. He decided not to ask any more questions for fear his ignorance might cost him the job. Whatever hunting involved, he and his body could surely handle it. And a job, any job, was as necessary now for his self-respect as for his dwindling wallet.

He thanked Franchel and left.

That evening he ate dinner in an inexpensive diner, and bought several magazines. He was elated at the knowledge of having found work, and sure that he was going to make a place for himself in this age.

His high spirits were dampened slightly when he glimpsed, on the way back to his hotel, a man standing in an alley watching him. The man had a white face and placid Buddha eyes, and his rough clothes hung on him like rags on a scarecrow.

It was the zombie.

Blaine hurried on to his hotel, refusing to anticipate trouble. After all, if a cat can look at a king, a zombie can look at a man, and where's the harm?

This reasoning didn't prevent him from having nightmares until dawn.

Early the next day, Blaine walked to 42nd Street and Park Avenue, to catch a bus to the briefing. While waiting, he noticed a disturbance on the other side of 42nd Street.

A man had stopped short in the middle of the busy pavement. He was laughing to himself, and people were beginning to edge away from him. He was in his fifties,

Blaine judged, dressed in quiet tweeds, bespectacled, and a little overweight. He carried a small briefcase and looked like ten million other businessmen.

Abruptly he stopped laughing. He unzipped his briefcase and removed from it two long, slightly curved daggers. He flung the briefcase away, and followed it with his glasses.

'Berserker!' someone cried.

The man plunged into the crowd, both daggers flashing. People started screaming, and the crowd scattered before him.

'Berserker, berserker!'

'Call the flathats!'

'Watch *out*, berserker!'

One man was down, clutching his torn shoulder and swearing. The berserker's face was fiery red now, and spittle came from his mouth. He waded deeper into the dense crowd, and people knocked each other down in their efforts to escape. A woman shrieked as she was pushed off balance, and her armload of parcels scattered across the pavement.

The berserker swiped at her left-handed, missed, and plunged deeper into the crowd.

Blue-uniformed police appeared, six or eight of them, sidearms out. 'Everybody down!' they shouted. 'Flatten! Everybody down!'

All traffic had stopped. The people in the berserker's path flung themselves to the pavement. On Blaine's side of the street, people were also getting down.

A freckled girl of perhaps twelve tugged at Blaine's arm. 'Come on, Mister, get down! You wanna get beamed?'

Blaine lay down beside her. The berserker had turned and was running back toward the policemen, screaming wordlessly and waving his knives.

Three of the policemen fired at once, their weapons throwing a pale yellowish beam which flared red when it struck the berserker. He screamed as his clothing began to smoulder, turned, and tried to escape.

A beam caught him square in the back. He flung both knives at the policemen and collapsed.

An ambulance dropped down with whirring blades and quickly loaded the berserker and his victims. The policemen began breaking up the crowd that had gathered around them.

'All right, folks, it's all over now. Move along!'

The crowd began to disperse. Blaine stood up and brushed himself off. 'What was that?' he asked.

'It was a berserker, silly,' the freckled girl said. 'Couldn't you *see*?'

'I saw. Do you have many?'

She nodded proudly. 'New York has more berserkers than any other city in the world except Manila where they're called amokers. But it's all the same thing. We have maybe fifty a year.'

'More,' a man said. 'Maybe seventy, eighty a year. But this one didn't do so good.'

A small group had gathered near Blaine and the girl. They were discussing the berserker much as Blaine had heard strangers in his own time discuss an automobile accident.

'How many did he get?'

'Only five, and I don't think he killed any of them.'

'His heart wasn't in it,' an old woman said. 'When I was a girl you couldn't stop them as easily as that. Strong they were.'

'Well, he picked a bad spot,' the freckled girl said. '42nd Street is filled with flathats. A berserker can't hardly get started before he's beamed.'

A big policeman came over. 'All right, folks, break it up. The fun's over, move along now.'

The group dispersed. Blaine caught his bus, wondering why fifty or more people chose to berserk in New York every year. Sheer nervous tension? A demented form of individualism? Adult delinquency?

It was one more of the things he would have to find out about the world of 2110.

15

The address was a penthouse high above Park Avenue in the Seventies. A butler admitted him to a spacious room where chairs had been set up in a long row. The dozen men occupying the chairs were a loud, tough, weatherbeaten bunch, carelessly dressed and ill at ease in such rarefied surroundings. Most of them knew each other.

'Hey, Otto! Back in the hunting game?'

'Yah. No money.'

'Knew you'd come back, old boy. Hi, Tim!'

'Hi, Bjorn. This is my last hunt.'

'Sure it is. Last 'til next time.'

'No, I mean it. I'm buying a seed-pressure farm in the North Atlantic Abyss. I just need a stake.'

'You'll drink up your stake.'

'Not this time.'

'Hey, Theseus! How's the throwing arm?'

'Good enough, Chico. Que tal?'

'Not too bad, kid.'

'There's Sammy Jones, always last in.'

'I'm on time, ain't I?'

'Ten minutes late. Where's your sidekick?'

'Sligo? Dead. That Asturias hunt.'

'Tough. Hereafter?'

'Not likely.'

A man entered the room and called out, 'Gentlemen, your attention please!'

He advanced to the center of the room and stood, hands on his hips, facing the row of hunters. He was a slender sinewy man of medium height, dressed in riding breeches and an open-necked shirt. He had a small, carefully tended moustache and startling blue eyes in a thin, tanned face. For a few seconds he looked the hunters over, while they coughed and shifted their feet uncomfortably.

At last he said, 'Good morning, gentlemen. I am Charles Hull, your employer and Quarry.' He gave them a smile of no warmth. 'First, gentlemen, a word concerning the legality of our proceedings. There has been some recent confusion about this. My lawyer has looked into the matter fully, and will explain. Mr. Jensen!'

A small, nervous-looking man came into the room, pressed his spectacles firmly against his nose and cleared his throat.

'Yes, Mr. Hull. Gentlemen, as to the present legality of the hunt: In accordance with the revised statutes to the Suicide Act of 2102, any man protected by Hereafter insurance has the right to select any death for himself, at any time and place, and by any means, as long as those means do not constitute cruel and unnatural abuse. The reason for this fundamental "right to die" is obvious: The courts do not recognize physical death as death *per se*, if said death does not involve the destruction of mind. Providing the mind survives, the death of the body is of no more moment, legally, than the sloughing of a fingernail. The body, by the latest Supreme Court decision, is considered an appendage of the mind, its creature, to be disposed of as the mind directs.'

During this explanation Hull had been pacing the room with quick, catlike steps. He stopped now and said, 'Thank you, Mr. Jensen. So there is no questioning my right to suicide. Nor is there any illegality in my selecting one or more persons such as yourselves to perform the act for me. And your own actions are considered legal under the Permitted Murder section of the Suicide Act. All well and good. The only legal question arises in a recent appendage to the Suicide Act.'

He nodded to Mr. Jensen.

'The appendage states,' Jensen said, 'that a man can select any death for himself, at any time and place, by any means, etcetera *so long as that death is not physically injurious to others*.'

'That,' said Hull, 'is the troublesome clause. Now, a hunt is a legal form of suicide. A time and place is arranged.

You, the hunters, chase me. I, the Quarry, flee. You catch me, kill me. Fine! Except for one thing.'

He turned to the lawyer. 'Mr. Jensen, you may leave the room. I do not wish to implicate you.'

After the lawyer had left, Hull said, 'The one problem remaining is, of course, the fact that I will be armed and trying my very best to kill *you*. Any of you. All of you. And *that* is illegal.'

Hull sank gracefully into a chair. 'The crime, however, is mine, not yours. I have employed you to kill me. You have no idea that I plan to protect myself, to retaliate. That is a legal fiction, but one which will save you from becoming possible accessories to the fact. If I am caught trying to kill one of you, the penalty will be severe. But I will not be caught. One of you will kill me, thus putting me beyond the reach of human justice. If I should be so unfortunate as to kill *all* of you, I shall complete my suicide in the old-fashioned manner, with poison. But that would be a disappointment to me. I trust you will not be so clumsy as to let that happen. Any questions?'

The hunters were murmuring among themselves:

'Slick fancy-talking bastard.'

'Forget it, all Quarries talk like that.'

'Think's he's better than us, him and his classy legal talk.'

'We'll see how good he talks with a bit of steel through him.'

Hull smiled coldly. 'Excellent. I believe the situation is clear. Now, if you please, tell me what your weapons are.'

One by one the hunters answered:

'Mace.'

'Net and Trident.'

'Spear.'

'Morning star.'

'Bola.'

'Scimitar.'

'Bayonetted rifle,' Blaine said when his turn came.

'Broadsword.'

'Battle-axe.'

'Saber.'

'Thank you, gentlemen,' Hull said. 'I will be armed with a rapier, naturally, and no armor. Our meeting will take place Sunday, at dawn, on my estate. The butler will give each of you a paper containing full instructions on how to get there. Let the bayonet man remain. Good morning to the rest of you.'

The hunters left. Hull said, 'Bayonetry is an unusual art. Where did you learn it?'

Blaine hesitated, then said, 'In the army, 1943 to 1945.'

'You're from the past?'

Blaine nodded.

'Interesting,' Hull said, with no particular sign of interest. 'Then this, I daresay, is your first hunt?'

'It is.'

'You appear a person of some intelligence. I suppose you have your reasons for choosing so hazardous and disreputable an employment?'

'I'm low on funds,' Blaine said, 'and I can't find anything else to do.'

'Of course,' Hull said, as though he had known it all along. 'So you turned to hunting. Yet hunting is not a thing merely to turn to; and hunting the beast Man is not for everyone. The trade calls for certain special abilities, not the least of which is the ability to kill. Do you think you have the innate talent?'

'I believe so,' Blaine said, though he hadn't considered the question until now.

'I wonder,' Hull mused. 'In spite of your bellicose appearance, you don't seem the type. What if you find yourself incapable of killing me? What if you hesitate at the crucial moment when steel grates on steel?'

'I'll chance it,' Blaine said.

Hull nodded agreeably. 'And so will I. Perhaps, hidden deep within you, a spark of murder burns. Perhaps not. This doubt will add spice to the game – though you may not have time to savour it.'

'That's my worry,' Blaine said, feeling an intense dislike for his elegant and rhetorical employer. 'Might I ask you a question?'

'Consider me at your service.'

'Thank you. Why do you wish to die?'

Hull stared at him, then burst into laughter. 'Now I *know* you're from the past! What a question!'

'Can you answer it?'

'Of course,' Hull said. He leaned back in his chair, and his eyes took on the dreamy look of a man forming rhetoric.

'I am forty-three years old, and weary of nights and days. I am a wealthy man, and an uninhibited one. I have experimented, contrived, laughed, wept, loved, hated, tasted and drunk – my fill. I have sampled all Earth has to offer me, and I choose not to tediously repeat the experience. When I was young, I pictured this excellent green planet revolving mysteriously around its flamboyant yellow luminary as a treasure-trove, a brass box of delights inexhaustible in content and immeasurable in their effect upon my ever-eager desires. But now, sadly, I have lived longer and have witnessed sensation's end. And now I see with what bourgeois complacency our fat round Earth circles, at wary distance and unvarying pace, its gaudy dreaded star. And the imagined treasure chest of the Earth seems now a child's painted toy box, shallow in its contents and mediocre in its effect upon nerves too quickly deadened to all delight.'

Hull glanced at Blaine to note the effect of his words, and then went on.

'Boredom stretches before me now like a vast arid plain – and I choose not to be bored. I choose, instead, to move on, move forward, move out; to sample Earth's last and greatest adventure – the adventure of Death, gateway to the afterlife. Can you understand that?'

'Of course,' Blaine said, irritated yet impressed by Hull's theatrics. 'But what's the rush? Life might have some good things still in store for you. And death is inevitable. Why rush it?'

'Spoken like a true 20th Century optimist,' Hull said, laughing. ' "Life is real, life is earnest . . ." In your day, one *had* to believe that life was real and earnest. What alternative was there? How many of you really believed in a life after death?'

91

'That doesn't alter the validity of my point,' Blaine said, hating the stodgy, cautious, reasonable position he was forced to assume.

'But it does! The perspective on life and death has changed now. Instead of Longfellow's prosy advice, we follow Nietzsche's dictum – to die at the right time! Intelligent people don't clutch at the last shreds of life like drowning men clinging to a bit of board. They know that the body's life is only an infinitesimal portion of man's total existence. Why shouldn't they speed the body's passing by a few years if they so desire? Why shouldn't those bright pupils skip a grade or two of school? Only the frightened, the stupid, the uneducated grasp at every possible monotonous second on Earth.'

'The frightened, stupid and uneducated,' Blaine repeated. 'And the unfortunates who can't afford Hereafter insurance.'

'Wealth and class have their privileges,' Hull said, smiling faintly, 'and their obligations as well. One of those obligations is the necessity of dying at the right time, before one becomes a bore to one's peers and a horror to oneself. But the deed of dying transcends class and breeding. It is every man's patent of nobility, his summons from the king, his knightly adventure, the greatest deed of his life. And how he acquits himself in that lonely and perilous enterprise is his true measure as a man.'

Hull's blue eyes were fierce and glittering. He said, 'I do not wish to experience this crucial event in bed. I do not wish a dull, tame, commonplace death to sneak over me disguised as sleep. I choose to die – fighting!'

Blaine nodded in spite of himself, and felt regret at his own prosaic death. A car accident! How dull, tame, and commonplace! And how strange, dark, atavistic and noble seemed Hull's lordly selection of death. Pretentious, of course; but then, life itself was a pretension in the vast universe of unliving matter. Hull was like an ancient Japanese nobleman calmly kneeling to perform the ceremonial act of hara-kiri and emphasizing the importance of life in the very selection of death. But hara-kiri was a passive

Eastern avowal; while Hull's manner of dying was a Western death, fierce, violent, exultant.

It was admirable. But intensely irritating to a man not yet prepared to die.

Blaine said, 'I have nothing against you or any other man choosing his death. But what about the hunters you plan to kill? They haven't chosen to die, and they won't survive in the hereafter.'

Hull shrugged his shoulders. 'They choose to live dangerously. In Nietzsche's phrase, they prefer to run risk and danger, and play dice with death. Blaine, have you changed your mind?'

'No.'

'Then we will meet Sunday.'

Blaine went to the door and took his paper of instructions from the butler. As he was leaving, he said, 'I wonder if you've considered one last thing.'

'What is that?' Hull asked.

'You must have thought of it,' Blaine said. 'The possibility that this whole elaborate setup – the scientific hereafter, voices of the dead, ghosts – are merely a gigantic hoax, a money-making fraud perpetrated by Hereafter, Inc.'

Hull stood perfectly still. When he spoke there was a hint of anger in his voice. 'That is *quite* impossible. Only a very uneducated man could think such a thing.'

'Maybe,' Blaine said. 'But wouldn't you look silly if it *were* a hoax! Good morning, Mr. Hull.'

He left, glad to have shaken up that smooth, smug, fancy, rhetorical bastard even for a moment – and sad that his own death had been so dull, tame, and commonplace.

16

The following day, Saturday, Blaine went to Franchel's apartment for his rifle, bayonet, hunter's uniform and pack. He was given half his salary in advance, less ten percent and the cost of the equipment. The money was very welcome, for he had been down to three dollars and change.

He went to the Spiritual Switchboard, but Melhill had left no further messages for him. He returned to his hotel room and spent the afternoon practicing lunges and parries.

That evening Blaine found himself tense and despondent, and nervous at the thought of the hunt beginning in the morning. He went to a small West Side cocktail lounge that had been designed to resemble a 20th Century bar, with a dark gleaming bar, wooden stools, booths, a brass rail, and sawdust on the floor. He slid into a booth and ordered beer.

The classic neon lights glowed softly, and a genuine antique juke box played the sentimental tunes of Glenn Miller and Benny Goodman. Blaine sat, hunched over his glass of beer, drearily asking himself who and what he was.

Was it truly *he* taking employment as a hunter and killer of men?

Then what happened to *Tom Blaine*, the former designer of sailboats, former listener to high-fidelity music, former reader of fine books, former viewer of good plays? What happened to that quiet, sardonic, non-aggressive man?

Surely that man, housed in his slender, nervous, unassuming body, would never choose to kill!

Would he?

Was that familiar and regretted Blaine defeated and smothered by the large, square-muscled, quick-reflexed fighter's body he had acquired? And was that body, with its own peculiar glandular secretions dripping into the dark bloodstream, its own distinct and configurated brain, its own system of nerves and signals and responses – was that domineering body responsible for everything, dragging its helpless owner into murderous violence?

Blaine rubbed his eyes and told himself that he was dreaming nonsense. The truth simply was: He had died through circumstances beyond his control, been reborn in the future, and found himself unemployable except as a hunter. Q.E.D.

But that rational explanation didn't satisfy him, and he no longer had time to search out the slippery and elusive truth.

He was no longer a detached observer of 2110. He had become a biased participant, an actor instead of an onlooker, with all of an actor's thoughtless sweep and rush. Action was irresistible, it generated its own momentary truth. The brakes were off, and the engine Blaine was rolling down the steep hill Life, gathering momentum but no moss. Perhaps this, now, was his last chance for a look, a summing up, a measured choice . . .

But it was already too late, for a man slid into the booth opposite him like a shadow across the world. And Blaine was looking into the white and impassive face of the zombie.

'Good evening,' the zombie said.

'Good evening,' Blaine said steadily. 'Would you care for a drink?'

'No, thank you. My system doesn't respond to stimulation.'

'Sorry to hear it,' Blaine said.

The zombie shrugged his shoulders. 'I have a name now,' he said. 'I decided to call myself Smith, until I remember my real name. Smith. Do you like it?'

'It's a fine name,' Blaine said.

'Thank you. I went to a doctor,' Smith said. 'He told me my body's no good. No stamina, no recuperative powers.'

'Can't you be helped?'

Smith shook his head. 'The body's definitely zombie. I occupied it much too late. The doctor gives me another few months at most.'

'Too bad,' Blaine said, feeling nausea rise in his throat at the sight of that sullen, thick-featured, leaden-skinned face with its unharmonious features and patient Buddha's eyes. Smith sat, slack and unnatural in rough workman's clothes, his black-dotted white face close-shaven and smelling of strong lotion. But he had changed. Already Blaine could see a certain leathery dryness in the once-pliant skin, certain striations in the flesh around the eyes, nose and mouth, minute creases in the forehead like tool-marks in old leather. And, mingled with the heavy after-shaving lotion, Blaine thought he could sense the first faint odor of dissolution.

'What do you want with me?' Blaine asked.

'I don't know.'

'Then leave me alone.'

'I can't do that,' Smith said apologetically.

'Do you want to kill me?' Blaine asked, his throat dry.

'I don't know! I can't remember! Kill you, protect you, maim you, love you – I don't know yet! But I'll remember soon, Blaine, I promise!'

'Leave me alone,' Blaine said, his muscles tensing.

'I can't,' Smith said. 'Don't you understand? I know nothing except you. Literally nothing! I don't know this world or any other, no person, face, mind or memory. You're my only landmark, the center of my existence, my only reason for living.'

'Stop it!'

'But it's true! Do you think I *enjoy* dragging this structure of flesh through the streets? What good is life with no hope before me and no memory behind me? Death is better! Life means filthy decaying flesh, and death is pure spirit! I've thought about it, dreamed about it, beautiful fleshless death! But one thing stops me. I have *you*, Blaine, to keep me going!'

'Get out of here,' Blaine said, nausea bitter in his mouth.

'*You*, my sun and moon, my stars, my Earth, my total universe, my life, my reason, my friend, enemy, lover, murderer, wife, father, child, husband –'

Blaine's fist shot out, striking Smith high on the

cheekbone. The zombie was flung back in the booth. His expression did not change, but a great purple bruise appeared on his lead-colored cheekbone.

'*Your* mark!' Smith murmured.

Blaine's fist, poised for another blow, dropped.

Smith stood up. 'I'm going. Take care of yourself, Blaine. Don't die yet! I need you. Soon I'll remember, and I'll come to you.'

Smith, his sullen, slack, bruised face impassive, left the bar.

Blaine ordered a double whiskey and sat for a long time over it, trying to still the shaking in his hands.

17

Blaine arrived at the Hull estate by rural jet-bus, an hour before dawn. He was dressed in a traditional hunter's uniform – khaki shirt and slacks, rubber-soled shoes and wide-brimmed hat. Slung over one shoulder was his field pack; over the other he carried his rifle and bayonet in a plastic bag.

A servant met him at the outer gate and led him to the low, rambling mansion. Blaine learned that the Hull estate consisted of ninety wooded acres in the Adirondack Mountains between Keene and Elizabethtown. Here, the servant told him, Hull's father had suicided at the age of fifty-one, taking the lives of six hunters with him before a saber man slashed his head off. Glorious death! Hull's uncle, on the other hand, had chosen to berserk in San Francisco, a city he had always loved. The police had to beam him twelve times before he dropped, and he took seven bystanders with him. The newspapers made much of the exploit, and accounts of it were preserved in the family scrapbook.

It just went to show, the garrulous old retainer pointed out, the difference in temperaments. Some, like the uncle, were friendly, fun-loving men who wanted to die in a crowd, attracting a certain amount of attention. Others, like the present Mr. Hull, were more given to the love of solitude and nature.

Blaine nodded politely to all this and was taken to a large, rustic room where the hunters were assembled, drinking coffee and honing a last razor edge to their weapons. Light flashed from the blued-steel broadsword and silvery battle-axe, wavered along the polished spearhead and glinted frostily from the diamond-points of the mace and morning star. At first glance, Blaine thought it looked like a scene from medieval times. But on second thought he decided it was more like a movie set.

'Pull up a chair, pal,' the axeman called. 'Welcome to the Benevolent Protective Society of Butchers, Slaughterhouse Men, and Killers-at-Large. I'm Sammy Jones, finest axeman in the Americas and probably Europe, too.'

Blaine sat down and was introduced to the other hunters. They represented half a dozen nationalities, although English was their common tongue.

Sammy Jones was a squat, black-haired, bull-shouldered man, dressed in patched and faded khakis, with several old hunting scars across his craggy, thick-browed face.

'First hunt?' he asked, glancing at Blaine's neatly pressed khakis.

Blaine nodded, removed his rifle from its plastic bag and fitted the bayonet to its end. He tested the locking mechanism, tightened the rifle's strap, and removed the bayonet again.

'Can you really use that thing?' Jones asked.

'Sure,' Blaine said, more confidently than he felt.

'Hope so. Guys like Hull have a nose for the weak sisters. They try to cut 'em out of the pack early.'

'How long does a hunt usually last?' Blaine asked.

'Well,' Jones said, 'longest I was ever on took eight days. That was Asturias, where my partner Sligo got his. Generally a good pack can pin down a Quarry in a day or two. Depends on how he wants to die. Some try to hang on as long as they can. They run to cover. They hide in caves and ravines, the dirty treacherous dogs, and you have to go in for them and chance a thrust in the face. That's how Sligo got it. But I don't think Hull's that way. He wants to die like a great big fire-eating he-man hero. So he'll stalk around and take chances, looking to see how many of us he can knock off with his pigsticker.'

'You sound as if you don't approve,' Blaine said.

Sammy Jones raised his bushy eyebrows. 'I don't hold with making a big fuss about dying. Here comes the hero himself.'

Hull entered the room, lean and elegant in khaki-colored silk, with a white silk bandanna knotted loosely around his neck. He carried a light pack, and strapped to one shoulder was a thin, wicked-looking rapier.

'Good morning, gentlemen,' he said. 'Weapons all honed, packs straight, shoelaces firmly tied? Excellent!'

Hull walked to a window and drew the curtains aside.

'Behold the first crack of dawn, a glorious streak in our eastern skies, harbinger of our fierce Lord Sun who rules the chase. I shall leave now. A servant will inform you when my half hour grace is done. Then you may pursue, and kill me upon sight. If you are able! The estate is fenced. I will remain within its confines, and so shall you.'

Hull bowed then walked quickly and gracefully out of the room.

'God, I hate these fancy birds!' Sammy Jones shouted, after the door was closed. 'They're all alike, every one of them. Acting so cool and casual, so goddamned *heroic*. If they only knew how bloody *silly* I think they are – me that's been on twenty-eight of these things.'

'Why do you hunt?' Blaine asked.

Sammy Jones shrugged. 'My father was an axeman, and he taught me the business. It's the only thing I know.'

'You could learn a different trade,' Blaine said.

'I suppose I could. The fact is, I *like* killing these aristocratic gentlemen. I hate every rich bastard among them with their lousy hereafter a poor man can't afford. I take pleasure in killing them, and if I had money I'd pay for the privilege.'

'And Hull enjoys killing poor men like you,' Blaine said. 'It's a sad world.'

'No, just an honest one,' Sammy Jones told him. 'Stand up, I'll fasten your pack on right.'

When that was done, Sammy Jones said, 'Look Tom, why don't you and me stick together on this hunt? Mutual protection, like?'

'*My* protection, you mean,' Blaine said.

'Nothing to be ashamed of,' Jones told him. 'Every skilled trade must be learned before it can be practiced. And what better man to learn from than myself, the finest of the fine?'

'Thanks,' Blaine said. 'I'll try to hold up my end, Sammy.'

'You'll do fine. Now, Hull's a fencer, be sure of it, and fencers have their little tricks which I'll explain as we go along. When he –'

At that moment a servant entered, carrying an old, ornate chronometer. When the second hand passed twelve, he looked sharply at the hunters.

'Gentlemen,' he said, 'the time of grace is passed. The chase may begin.'

The hunters trooped outside into the grey, misty dawn. Theseus the tracker, balancing his trident across his shoulders, picked up the trail at once. It led upwards, toward a mist-wreathed mountain.

Spread out in a long single file, the hunters started up the mountain's side.

Soon the early morning sun had burned away the mists. Theseus lost the trail when it crossed bare granite. The hunters spread out in a broken line across the face of the mountain, and continued to advance slowly upward.

At noon, the broadsword man picked a fragment of khaki-colored silk from a thornbush. A few minutes later, Theseus found footprints on moss. They led down, into a narrow thickly wooded valley. Eagerly the hunters pressed forward.

'Here he is!' a man shouted.

Blaine whirled and saw, fifty yards to his right, the man with the morning star running forward. He was the youngest of the hunters, a brawny, self-confident Sicilian. His weapon consisted of a stout handle of ash, fixed to which was a foot of chain. At the end of the chain was a heavy spiked ball, the morning star. He was whirling this weapon over his head and singing at the top of his lungs.

Sammy Jones and Blaine sprinted toward him. They saw Hull break from the bushes, rapier in hand. The Sicilian leaped forward and swung a blow that could have felled a tree. Hull dodged lightly out of the way, and lunged.

The morning star man gurgled and went down, pierced through the throat. Hull planted a foot on his chest, yanked the rapier free, and vanished again into the underbrush.

'I never could understand why a man'd use a morning star,' Sammy Jones said. 'Too clumsy. If you don't hit your man the first lick, you never recover in time.'

The Sicilian was dead. Hull's passage through the underbrush was clearly visible. They plunged in after him, followed by most of the hunters, with flankers ranged on either side.

Soon they encountered rock again, and the trail was lost.

All afternoon they searched, with no luck. At sundown they pitched camp on the mountainside, posted guards, and discussed the day's hunting over a small campfire.

'Where do you suppose he is?' Blaine asked.

'He could be anywhere on the damned estate,' Jones said. 'Remember, he knows every foot of ground here. We're seeing it for the first time.'

'Then he could hide from us indefinitely.'

'If he wanted to. But he wants to be killed, remember? In a big, flashy, heroic way. So he'll keep on trying to cut us down until we get him.'

Blaine looked over his shoulder at the dark woods. 'He could be standing there now, listening.'

'No doubt he is,' Jones said. 'I hope the guards stay awake.'

Conversation droned on in the little camp, and the fire burned low. Blaine wished morning would come. Darkness reversed the roles. The hunters were the hunted now, stalked by a cruel and amoral suicide intent upon taking as many lives with him as possible.

With that thought, he dozed off.

Sometime before dawn he was awakened by a scream. Grabbing his rifle, he sprang to his feet and peered into the darkness. There was another scream, closer this time, and the sound of hurried movement through the woods. Then someone threw a handful of leaves on the dying fire.

In the sudden yellow glow, Blaine saw a man staggering back to the camp. It was one of the guards, trailing his spear behind him. He was bleeding in two places, but his wounds didn't appear fatal.

102

'That bastard,' the spearman sobbed, 'that lousy bastard.'

'Take it easy, Chico,' one of the men said, ripping open the spearman's shirt to clean and bandage the wound. 'Did you get him?'

'He was too quick,' the spearman moaned. 'I missed.'

That was the end of the sleeping for the night.

The hunters were moving again at the first light of dawn, widely scattered, looking for a trace of the Quarry. Theseus found a broken button and then a half-erased footprint. The hunt veered again, winding up a narrow-faced mountain.

At the head of the pack, Otto gave a sudden shout. 'Hey! Here! I got him!'

Theseus rushed toward him, followed by Blaine and Jones. They saw Hull backing away, watching intently as Otto advanced swinging the bola around his cropped head. The Argentinian lasso hissed in the air, its three iron balls blurring. Then Otto released it. Instantly Hull flung himself to the ground. The bola snaked through the air inches above his head, wrapped itself around a tree limb and snapped it off. Hull, grinning broadly, ran toward the weaponless man.

Before he could reach him Theseus had arrived, flourishing his trident. They exchanged thrusts. Then Hull whirled and ran.

Theseus lunged. The Quarry howled with pain but continued running.

'Did you wound him?' Jones asked.

'A flesh wound in the rump,' Theseus said. 'Probably most painful to his pride.'

The hunters ran on, panting heavily, up the mountain's side. But they had lost the Quarry again.

They spread out, surrounding the narrowing mountain, and slowly began working their way toward the peak. Occasional noises and footprints told them the Quarry was still before them, retreating upward. As the peak narrowed they were able to close their ranks more, lessening any chance of Hull slipping through.

By late afternoon the pine and spruce trees had become sparse. Above them was a confused labyrinth of granite boulders, and past that the final peak itself.

'Careful now!' Jones called to the hunters.

As he said it, Hull launched an attack. Springing from behind a rock pinnacle, he came at old Bjorn the mace man, his rapier hissing, trying to cut the man down quickly and escape the throttling noose of hunters.

But Bjorn gave ground only slowly, cautiously parrying the rapier thrusts, both hands on his mace as though it were a quarterstaff. Hull swore angrily at the phlegmatic man, attacked furiously, and threw himself aside just in time to avoid a blow of the mace.

Old Bjorn closed – too rapidly. The rapier darted in and out of his chest like a snake's flickering tongue. Bjorn's mace dropped, and his body began rolling down the mountainside.

But the hunters had closed the circle again. Hull retreated upward, into a maze of boulders.

The hunters pressed forward. Blaine noticed that the sun was almost down; already there was a twilight hue to the air, and long shadows stretched across the gray rocks.

'Getting toward evening,' he said to Jones.

'Maybe half an hour more light,' Jones said, squinting at the sky. 'We better get him soon. After dark he could pick every man of us off this rock.'

They moved more quickly now, searching among the high boulders.

'He could roll rocks on us,' Blaine said.

'Not him,' Jones said. 'He's too damn proud.'

And then Hull stepped from behind a high rock near Blaine.

'All right, rifleman,' he said.

Blaine, his rifle at high port, just managed to parry the thrust. The blade of the rapier rasped along the gun barrel, past his neck. Automatically he deflected it. Something drove him to roar as he lunged, to follow the lunge with an eager disembowelling slash and then a hopeful butt stroke intended to scatter his enemy's brains across the rocks. For that moment, Blaine was no longer a civilized man operating under a painful necessity; he was a more basic creature joyously pursuing his true vocation of murder.

The Quarry avoided his blows with quick silken grace. Blaine stumbled after him, anger sapping his skill. Suddenly he was shoved aside by Sammy Jones.

'Mine,' Jones said. 'All mine. I'm your boy, Hull. Try me with the pigsticker.'

Hull, his face expressionless, advanced, his rapier flashing. Jones stood firm on slightly bowed legs, the battleaxe turning lightly in his hands. Hull feinted and lunged. Jones parried so hard that sparks flew, and the rapier bent like a green stick.

The other hunters had come up now. They chose seats on nearby rocks and caught their wind, commenting on the duel and shouting advice.

'Pin him against the cliff, Sammy!'

'No, over the edge with him!'

'Want some help?'

'Hell no!' Jones shouted back.

'Watch out he don't nip a finger, Sammy.'

'Don't worry,' Jones said.

Blaine watched, his rage ebbing as quickly as it had come. He had assumed that a battleaxe would be a clumsy weapon requiring a full backswing for each stroke. But Sammy Jones handled the short, heavy axe as though it were a baton. He took no backswing but let drive from any position, recovering instantly, his implacable weight and drive forcing Hull toward the cliff's sheer edge. There was no real comparison between the two men, Blaine realized. Hull was a gifted amateur, a dilettante murderer; Jones was a seasoned professional killer. It was like matching a ferocious house dog against a jungle tiger.

The end came quickly in the blue twilight of the mountaintop. Sammy Jones parried a thrust and stamped forward, swinging his axe backhanded. The blade bit deep into Hull's left side. Hull fell screaming down the mountain's side. For seconds afterward they heard his body crash and turn.

'Mark where he lies,' Sammy Jones said.

'He's gotta be dead,' the saber man said.

'He probably is. But it isn't a workmanlike job unless we make sure.'

On the way down they found Hull's mangled and lifeless body. They marked the location for the burial party and walked on to the estate.

18

The hunters returned to the city in a group and threw a wild celebration. During the evening, Sammy Jones asked Blaine if he would join him on the next job.

'I've got a nice deal lined up in Omsk,' Jones said. 'A Russian nobleman wants to hold a couple of gladiatorial games. You'd have to use a spear, but it's the same as a rifle. I'd train you on the way. After Omsk, there's a really big hunt being organized in Manila. Five brothers want to suicide together. They want fifty hunters to cut them down. What do you say, Tom?'

Blaine thought carefully before answering. The hunter's life was the most compatible he had found so far in this world. He liked the rough companionship of men like Sammy Jones, the straight, simple thinking, the life outdoors, the action that erased all doubts.

On the other hand there was something terribly pointless about wandering around the world as a paid killer, a modern and approved version of the bully, the bravo, the thug. There was something futile about action just for action's sake, with no genuine intent or purpose behind it, no resolution or discovery. These considerations might not arise if he were truly what his body seemed; but he was not. The hiatus existed, and had to be faced.

And finally there were other problems that this world presented, other challenges more apropos to his personality. And those had to be met.

'Sorry, Sammy,' he said.

Jones shook his head. 'You're making a mistake, Tom. You're a natural-born killer. There's nothing else for you.'

'Perhaps now,' Blaine said, 'I have to find out.'

'Well, good luck,' Sammy Jones said. 'And take care of that body of yours. You picked a good one.'

Blaine blinked involuntarily. 'Is it so obvious?'

Jones grinned. 'I been around, Tom. I can tell when a man is wearing a host. If your mind had been *born* in that body, you'd be away and hunting with me. And if your mind had been born in a different body –'

'Yes?'

'You wouldn't have gone hunting in the first place. It's a bad splice, Tom. You'd better figure out which way you're going.'

'Thanks,' Blaine said. They shook hands and Blaine left for his hotel.

He reached his room and flung himself, fully dressed, upon the bed. When he awoke he would call Marie. But first, he had to sleep. All plans, thoughts, problems, decisions, even dreams, would have to wait. He was tired down to the very bone.

He snapped off the lights. Within seconds he was asleep.

Several hours later he awoke with a sensation of something wrong. The room was dark. Everything was still, more silent and expectant than New York had any right to be.

He sat upright in bed and heard a faint movement on the other side of the room, near the washbasin.

Blaine reached out and snapped on the light. There was no one in the room. But as he watched, his enamelled washbasin rose in the air. Slowly it lifted, hovering impossibly without support. And at the same time he heard a thin shattering laugh.

He knew at once he was being haunted, and by a poltergeist.

Carefully he eased out of bed and moved toward the door. The suspended basin dipped suddenly and plunged toward his head. He ducked, and the basin shattered against the wall.

His water pitcher levitated now, followed by two heavy tumblers. Twisting and turning erratically, they edged toward him.

Blaine picked up a pillow as a shield and rushed to the door. He turned the lock as a tumbler shattered above his

108

head. The door wouldn't open. The poltergeist was holding it shut.

The pitcher struck him violently in the ribs. The remaining tumbler buzzed in an ominous circle around his head, and he was forced to retreat from the door.

He remembered the fire escape outside his window. But the poltergeist thought of it as he started to move. The curtains suddenly burst into flame. At the same instant the pillow he was holding caught fire, and Blaine threw it from him.

'Help!' he shouted. 'Help!'

He was being forced into a corner of the room. With a rumble the bed slid forward, blocking his retreat. A chair rose slowly into the air and poised itself for a blow at his head.

And continually there was a thin and shattering laughter that Blaine could almost recognize.

PART THREE

19

As the bed crept toward him Blaine shouted for help in a voice that made the window rattle. His only answer was the poltergeist's high-pitched laugh.

Were they all deaf in the hotel? Why didn't someone answer?

Then he realized that, by the very nature of things, no one would even consider helping him. Violence was a commonplace in this world, and a man's death was entirely his own business. There would be no inquiry. The janitor would simply clean up the mess in the morning, and the room would be marked vacant.

His door was impassable. The only chance he could see was to jump over the bed and through the closed window. If he made the leap properly, he would fall against the waist-high fire escape railing outside. If he jumped too hard he would go right over the railing, and fall three stories to the street.

The chair beat him over the shoulders, and the bed rumbled forward to pin him against the wall. Blaine made a quick calculation of angles and distances, drew himself together and flung himself at the window.

He hit squarely; but he had reckoned without the advances of modern science. The window bent outward like a sheet of rubber, and snapped back into place. He was thrown against a wall, and fell dazed to the floor. Looking up, he saw a heavy bureau wobble toward him and slowly tilt.

As the poltergeist threw his lunatic strength against the bureau, the unwatched door swung open. Smith entered the room, his thick-featured zombie face impassive, and deflected the falling bureau with his shoulder.

'Come on,' he said.

Blaine asked no questions. He scrambled to his feet and

grabbed the edge of the closing door. With Smith's help he pulled it open again, and the two men slipped out. From within the room he heard a shriek of baffled rage.

Smith hurried down the hall, one cold hand clasped around Blaine's wrist. They went downstairs, through the hotel lobby and into the street. The zombie's face was leaden white except for the purple bruise where Blaine had struck him. The bruise had spread across nearly half his face, piebalding it into a Harlequin's grotesque mask.

'Where are we going?' Blaine asked.

'To a safe place.'

They reached an ancient unused subway entrance, and descended. One flight down they came to a small iron door set in the cracked concrete door. Smith opened the door and beckoned Blaine to follow him.

Blaine hesitated, and caught the hint of high-pitched laughter. The poltergeist was pursuing him, as the Eumenides had once pursued their victims through the streets of ancient Athens. He could stay in the lighted upper world if he wished, hag-ridden by the insane spirit. Or he could descend with Smith, through the iron door and into the darkness beyond it, to some uncertain destiny in the underworld.

The shrill laughter increased. Blaine hesitated no longer. He followed Smith through the iron door and closed it behind him.

For the moment, the poltergeist had chosen not to pursue. They walked down a tunnel lighted by an occasional naked light bulb, past cracked masonry pipes and the looming gray corpse of a subway train, past rusted iron cables lying in giant serpent coils. The air was moist and rank, and a thin slime underfoot made walking treacherous.

'Where are we going?' Blaine asked.

'To where I can protect you,' Smith said.

'Can you?'

'Spirits aren't invulnerable. Exorcism is possible if the true identity of the ghost is known.'

'Then you know who is haunting me?'

'I think so. There's only one person it logically could be.'
'Who?'

Smith shook his head. 'I'd rather not say his name yet. No sense calling him if he's not here.'

They descended a series of crumbling shale steps into a wider chamber, and circled the edge of a small black pond whose surface looked as hard and still as jet. On the other side of the pond was a passageway. A man stood in front of it, blocking the way.

He was a tall husky Negro, dressed in rags, armed with a length of iron pipe. From his look Blaine knew he was a zombie.

'This is my friend,' Smith said. 'May I bring him through?'

'You sure he's no inspector?'

'Absolutely sure.'

'Wait here,' the Negro said. He disappeared into the passageway.

'Where are we?' Blaine asked.

'Underneath New York, in a series of unused subway tunnels, old sewer conduits, and some passageways we've fashioned for ourselves.'

'But why did we come here?' Blaine asked.

'Where else would we go?' Smith asked, surprised. 'This is my home. Didn't you know? You're in New York's zombie colony.'

Blaine didn't consider a zombie colony much improvement over a ghost; but he didn't have time to think about it. The Negro returned. With him was a very old man who walked with the aid of a stick. The man's face was broken into a network of a thousand lines and wrinkles. His eyes barely showed through the fine scrollwork of sagging flesh, and even his lips were wrinkled.

'This is the man you told me about?' he asked.

'Yes sir,' said Smith. 'This is the man. Blaine, let me introduce you to Mr. Kean, the leader of our colony. May I take him through, sir?'

'You may,' the old man said. 'And I will accompany you for a while.'

They started down the passageway, Mr. Kean supporting himself heavily on the Negro's arm.

'In the usual course of events,' Mr. Kean said, 'only zombies are allowed in the colony. All others are barred. But it has been years since I spoke with a normal, and I thought the experience might be valuable. Therefore, at Smith's earnest request, I made an exception in your case.'

'I'm very grateful,' Blaine said, hoping he had reason to be.

'Don't misunderstand me. I am not averse to helping you. But first and foremost I am responsible for the safety of the eleven hundred zombies living beneath New York. For their sake, normals must be kept out. Exclusivity is our only hope in an ignorant world.' Mr. Kean paused. 'But perhaps you can help us, Blaine.'

'How?'

'By listening and understanding, and passing on what you have learned. Education is our only hope. Tell me, what do you know about the problems of a zombie?'

'Very little.'

'I will instruct you. Zombieism, Mr. Blaine, is a disease which has long had a powerful aura of superstition surrounding it, comparable to the aura generated by such diseases as epilepsy, leprosy, or St. Vitus' Dance. The spiritualizing tendency is a common one. Schizophrenia, you know, was once thought to mean possession by devils, and hydrocephalic idiots were considered peculiarly blessed. Similar fantasies attach to zombieism.'

They walked in silence for a few moments. Mr. Kean said, 'The superstition of the zombie is essentially Haitian; the disease of the zombie is worldwide, although rare. But the superstition and the disease have become hopelessly confused in the public mind. The zombie of superstition is an element of the Haitian Vodun cult; a human being whose soul has been stolen by magic. The zombie's body could be used as the magician wished, could even be slaughtered and sold for meat in the marketplace. If the zombie ate salt or beheld the sea, he realized he was dead and returned to his grave. For all this, there is no basis in fact.

116

'The superstition arose from the descriptively similar disease. Once it was exceedingly rare. But today, with the increase in mind-switching and reincarnation techniques, zombieism has become more common. The *disease* of the zombie occurs when a mind occupies a body that has been untenanted too long. Mind and body are not then one, as yours are, Mr. Blaine. They exist, instead, as quasi-independent entities engaged in an uneasy cooperation. Take our friend Smith as typical. He can control his body's gross physical actions, but fine coordination is impossible for him. His voice is incapable of discrete modulation, and his ears do not receive subtle differences in tone. His face is expressionless, for he has little or no control over his surface musculature. He drives his body, but is not truly a part of it.'

'And can't anything be done?' Blaine asked.

'At the present time, nothing.'

'I'm very sorry,' Blaine said uncomfortably.

'This is not a plea for your sympathy,' Kean told him. 'It is a request only for the most elementary understanding. I simply want you and everyone to know that zombieism is not a visitation of sins, but a *disease*, like mumps or cancer, and nothing more.'

Mr. Kean leaned against the wall of the passageway to catch his breath. 'To be sure, the zombie's appearance is unpleasant. He shambles, his wounds never heal, his body deteriorates rapidly. He mumbles like an idiot, staggers like a drunk, stares like a pervert. But is this any reason to make him the repository of all guilt and shame upon Earth, the leper of the 22nd century? They say that zombies attack people; yet his body is fragile in the extreme, and the average zombie couldn't resist a child's determined assault. They believe the disease is communicable; and this is obviously not so. They say that zombies are sexually perverted, and the truth is that a zombie experiences no sexual feelings whatsoever. But people refuse to learn, and zombies are outcasts fit only for the hangman's noose or the lyncher's burning stake.'

'What about the authorities?' Blaine asked.

Mr. Kean smiled bitterly. 'They used to lock us up, as a kindness, in mental institutions. You see, they didn't want us hurt. Yet zombies are rarely insane, and the authorities knew it! So now, with their tacit approval, we occupy these abandoned subway tunnels and sewer lines.'

'Couldn't you find a better place?' Blaine asked.

'Frankly, the underground suits us. Sunlight is bad for unregenerative skins.'

They began walking again. Blaine said, 'What can I do?'

'You can tell someone what you learned here. Write about it, perhaps. Widening ripples . . .'

'I'll do what I can.'

'Thank you,' Mr. Kean said gravely. 'Education is our only hope. Education and the future. Surely people will be more enlightened in the future.'

The future? Blaine felt suddenly dizzy. For *this* was the future, to which he had travelled from the idealistic and hopeful 20th century. *Now* was the future! But the promised enlightenment still had not come, and people were much the same as ever. For a second Blaine's centuries pressed heavily on him. He felt disoriented and old, older than Kean, older than the human race – a creature in a borrowed body standing in a place it did not know.

'And now,' Mr. Kean said, 'we have reached your destination.'

Blaine blinked rapidly, and life came back into focus. The dim passageway had ended. In front of him was a rusted iron ladder fastened to the tunnel wall, leading upward into darkness.

'Good luck,' Mr. Kean said. He left, supporting himself heavily on the Negro's arm. Blaine watched the old man go, then turned to Smith.

'Where are we going?'

'Up the ladder.'

'But where does it lead?'

Smith had already begun climbing. He stopped and looked down, his lead-colored lips drawn back into a grin. 'We're going to visit a friend of yours, Blaine. We're going to his tomb, up to his coffin, and ask him to stop haunting you. Force him, maybe.'

'Who is he?' Blaine asked.

Smith only grinned and continued climbing. Blaine mounted the ladder behind him.

Above the passageway was a ventilation shaft, which led to another passageway. They came at last to a door, and entered.

They were in a large, brilliantly lighted room. Upon the arched ceiling was a mural depicting a handsome clear-eyed man entering a gauzy blue heaven in the company of angels. Blaine knew at once who had modeled for the painting.

'Reilly!'

Smith nodded. 'We're inside his Palace of Death.'

'How did you know Reilly was haunting me?'

'You should have thought of it yourself. Only two people connected with you have died recently. The ghost certainly was not Ray Melhill. It had to be Reilly.'

'But why?'

'I don't know,' Smith said. 'Perhaps Reilly will tell you himself.'

Blaine looked at the walls. They were inlaid with crosses, crescent moons, stars and swastikas, as well as Indian, African, Arabian, Chinese and Polynesian good-luck signs. On pedestals around the room were statues of ancient deities. Among the dozens Blaine recognized Zeus, Apollo, Dagon, Odin and Astarte. In front of each pedestal was an altar, and on each altar was a cut and polished jewel.

'What's that for?' Blaine asked.

'Propitiation.'

'But life after death is a scientific fact.'

'Mr. Kean told me that science has little effect upon superstition,' Smith said. 'Reilly was fairly sure he'd survive after death; but he saw no reason to take chances. Also, Mr. Kean says that the very rich, like the very religious, wouldn't enjoy a hereafter filled with just *anybody*. They think that, by suitable rites and symbols, they can get into a more exclusive part of the hereafter.'

'Is there a more exclusive part?' Blaine asked.

'No one knows. It's just a belief.'

Smith led him across the room to an ornate door covered with Egyptian hieroglyphics and Chinese ideograms.

'Reilly's body is inside here,' Smith said.

'And we're going in?'

'Yes, we have to.'

Smith pushed the door open. Blaine saw a vast marble-pillared room. In its very center was a bronze and gold coffin inlaid with jewels. Surrounding the coffin was a great and bewildering quantity of goods; paintings and sculptures, musical instruments, carvings, objects like washing machines, stoves, refrigerators, even a complete helicopter. There was clothing and books, and a lavish banquet had been laid out.

'What's all this stuff for?' Blaine asked.

'The essence of these goods is intended to accompany the owner into the hereafter. It's an old belief.'

Blaine's first reaction was one of pity. The scientific hereafter hadn't freed men from the fear of death, as it should have done. On the contrary, it had intensified their uncertainties and stimulated their competitive drive. Given the surety of an afterlife, man wanted to improve upon it, to enjoy a better heaven than anyone else. Equality was all very well; but individual initiative came first. A perfect and passionless levelling was no more palatable an idea in the hereafter than it was on Earth. The desire to surpass caused a man like Reilly to build a tomb like the Pharaohs of ancient Egypt, to brood all his life about death, to live continually trying to find ways of preserving his property and status in the gray uncertainties ahead.

A shame. And yet, Blaine thought, wasn't his pity based upon a lack of belief in the efficacy of Reilly's measures? Suppose you *could* improve your situation in the hereafter? In that case, what better way to spend one's time on Earth than working for a better eternity?

The proposition seemed reasonable, but Blaine refused to believe it. *That* couldn't be the only reason for existence on Earth! Good or bad, fair or foul, the thing had to be lived for its own sake.

Smith walked slowly into the coffin room, and Blaine stopped his speculations. The zombie stood, contemplating a small table covered with ornaments. Dispassionately he kicked the table over. Then slowly, one by one, he ground the delicate ornaments into the polished marble floor.

'What are you doing?' Blaine asked.

'You want the poltergeist to leave you alone?'

'Of course.'

'Then he must have some *reason* for leaving you alone,' Smith said, kicking over an elaborate ebony sculpture.

It seemed reasonable enough to Blaine. Even a ghost must know he will eventually leave the Threshold and enter the hereafter. When he does, he wants his goods waiting for him, intact. Therefore fight fire with fire, persecution with persecution.

Still, he felt like a vandal when he picked up an oil painting and prepared to shove his fist through it.

'Don't,' said a voice above his head.

Blaine and Smith looked up. Above them there seemed to be a faint silvery mist. From the mist an attenuated voice said, 'Please put down the painting.'

Blaine held on to it, his fist poised. 'Are you Reilly?'

'Yes.'

'Why are you haunting me?'

'Because you're responsible! Everything's your fault! You killed me with your evil murdering mind! Yes *you*, you hideous thing from the past, you damned monster!'

'I didn't!' Blaine cried.

'You did! You aren't human! You aren't natural! Everything shuns you except your friend the dead man! Why aren't *you* dead, murderer?'

Blaine's fist moved toward the painting. The thin voice screamed, 'Don't!'

'Will you leave me alone?' Blaine asked.

'Put down the painting,' Reilly begged.

Blaine put it carefully down.

'I'll leave you alone,' Reilly said. 'Why shouldn't I?

122

There are things you can't see, Blaine, but *I* see them. Your time on Earth will be short, very short, painfully short. Those you trust will betray you, those you hate will conquer you. You will die, Blaine, not in years but soon, sooner than you can believe. You'll be betrayed, and you'll die by your own hand.'

'You're crazy!' Blaine shouted.

'Am I?' Reilly cackled. 'Am I? *Am I?*'

The silvery mist vanished. Reilly was gone.

Smith led him back through narrow winding passageways to the street level. Outside the air was chilly, and dawn had touched the tall buildings with red and gray.

Blaine started to thank him, but Smith shook his head. 'No reason for thanks! After all, I need you, Blaine. Where would I be if the poltergeist killed you? Take care of yourself, be careful. Nothing is possible for me without you.'

The zombie gazed anxiously at him for a moment, then hurried away. Blaine watched him go, wondering if it wouldn't be better to have a dozen enemies than Smith for a friend.

21

Half an hour later he was at Marie Thorne's apartment. Marie, without makeup, dressed in a housecoat, blinked sleepily and led him to the kitchen, where she dialed coffee, toast and scrambled eggs.

'I wish,' she said, 'you'd make your dramatic appearances at a decent hour. It's six-thirty in the morning.'

'I'll try to do better in the future,' Blaine said cheerfully.

'You said you'd call. What happened to you?'

'Did you worry?'

'Not in the slightest. What happened?'

Between bites of toast Blaine told her about the hunt, the haunting, and the exorcism. She listened to it all, then said, 'So you're obviously very proud of yourself, and I guess you should be. But you still don't know what Smith wants from you, or even who he is.'

'Haven't the slightest idea,' Blaine said. 'Smith doesn't, either. Frankly, I couldn't care less.'

'What happens when he finds out?'

'I'll worry about that when it happens.'

Marie raised both eyebrows but made no comment. 'Tom, what are your plans now?'

'I'm going to get a job.'

'As a hunter?'

'No. Logical or not, I'm going to try the yacht design agencies. Then I'm going to come around here and bother you at reasonable hours. How does that sound?'

'Impractical. Do you want some good advice?'

'No.'

'I'm giving it to you anyhow. Tom, get out of New York. Go as far away as you can. Go to Fiji or Samoa.'

'Why should I?'

Marie began to pace restlessly up and down the kitchen. 'You simply don't understand this world.'

'I think I do.'

'No! Tom, you've had a few typical experiences, that's all. But that doesn't mean you've assimilated our culture. You've been snatched, haunted, and you've gone on a hunt. But it adds up to not much more than a guided tour. Reilly was right, you're as lost and helpless as a caveman would be in your own 1958.'

'That's ridiculous, and I object to the comparison.'

'All right, let's make it a 14th century Chinese. Suppose this hypothetical Chinaman had met a gangster, gone on a bus ride and seen Coney Island. Would you say he understood 20th century America?'

'Of course not. But what's the point?'

'The point,' she said, 'is that you aren't safe here, and you can't even sense what or where or how urgent the dangers are. For one, that damned Smith is after you. Next, Reilly's heirs might not take kindly to you desecrating his tomb; they might find it necessary to do something about it. And the directors at Rex are still arguing about what *they* should do about you. You've altered things, changed things, disrupted things. Can't you *feel* it?'

'I can handle Smith,' Blaine said. 'To hell with Reilly's heirs. As for the directors, what can they do to me?'

She came over to him and put her arms around his neck. 'Tom,' she said earnestly, 'any man born here who found himself in your shoes would run as fast as he could!'

Blaine held her close for a moment and stroked her sleek dark hair. She cared for him, she wanted him to be safe. But he was in no mood for warnings. He had survived the dangers of the hunt, had passed through the iron door into the underworld and won through again to the light. Now, sitting in Marie's sunny kitchen, he felt elated and at peace with the world. Danger seemed an academic problem not worthy of discussion at the moment, and the idea of running away from New York was absurd.

'Tell me,' Blaine said lightly, 'among the things I've disrupted – is one of them you?'

'I'm probably going to lose my job, if that's what you mean.'

'That's not what I mean.'

'Then you should know the answer . . . Tom, will you please get out of New York?'

'No. And please stop sounding so panicky.'

'Oh Lord,' she sighed. 'We talk the same language but I'm not getting through. You don't understand. Let me try an example.' She thought for a moment. 'Suppose a man owned a sailboat –'

'Do you sail?' Blaine asked.

'Yes, I love sailing. Tom, listen to me! Suppose a man owned a sailboat in which he was planning an ocean voyage –'

'Across the sea of life,' Blaine filled in.

'You're not funny,' she said, looking very pretty and serious. 'This man doesn't know anything about boats. He sees it floating, nicely painted, everything in place. He can't imagine any danger. Then *you* look the boat over. You see that the frames are cracked, teredos have gotten into the rudder post, there's dry rot in the mast step, the sails are mildewed, the keel bolts are rusted, and the fastenings are ready to let go.'

'Where'd you learn so much about boats?' Blaine asked.

'I've been sailing since I was a kid. Will you please pay attention? You tell that man his boat is not seaworthy, the first gale is likely to sink him.'

'We'll have to go sailing sometime,' Blaine said.

'But this man,' Marie continued doggedly, 'doesn't know anything about boats. The thing *looks* all right. And the hell of it is, you can't tell him exactly what's going to happen, or when. Maybe the boat will hold together for a month, or a year, or maybe only a week. Maybe the keel bolts will go first, or perhaps it'll be the mast. You just don't know. And that's the situation here. I can't tell you what's going to happen, or when. I just know you're unseaworthy. You *must* get out of here!'

She looked at him hopefully. Blaine nodded and said, 'You'll make one hell of a crew.'

'So you're not going?'

'No. I've been up all night. The only place I'm going now is to bed. Would you care to join me?'

'Go to hell!'

'Darling, please! Where's your pity for a homeless wanderer from the past?'

'I'm going out,' she said. 'Help yourself to the bedroom. You'd better think about what I told you.'

'Sure,' Blaine said. 'But why should I worry when I have you looking out for me?'

'Smith's looking for you, too,' she reminded him. She kissed him quickly and left the room.

Blaine finished his breakfast and turned in. He awoke in the early afternoon. Marie still hadn't returned, so before leaving he wrote her a cheerful note with the address of his hotel.

During the next few days he visited most of the yacht design agencies in New York, without success. His old firm, Mattison & Peters, was long defunct. The other firms weren't interested. Finally, at Jaakobsen Yachts, Ltd., the head designer questioned him closely about the now-extinct Chesapeake Bay and Bahamas work boats. Blaine demonstrated his considerable knowledge of the types, as well as his out-of-date draftsmanship.

'We get a few calls for antique hulls,' the head designer said. 'Tell you what. We'll hire you as office boy. You can do classic hulls on a commission basis and study up on your designing, which, frankly, is old-fashioned. When you're ready, we'll upgrade you. What do you say?'

It was an inferior position; but it was a job, a legitimate job, with a fine chance for advancement. It meant that at last he had a real place in the world of 2110.

'I'll take it,' Blaine said, 'with thanks.'

That evening, by way of celebrating, he went to a Sensory Shop to buy a player and a few recordings. He was entitled, he thought, to a little basic luxury.

The sensories were an inescapable part of 2110, as omnipresent and popular as television had been in Blaine's day. Larger and more elaborate versions of the sensories were used for theater productions, and variations were employed for advertising and propaganda. They were to date the purest and most powerful form of the ready-made dream, tailored to fit anyone.

But they had their extremely vocal opponents, who deplored the ominous trend toward complete passivity in the spectator. These critics were disturbed by the excessive ease with which a person could assimilate a sensory; and in truth, many a housewife walked blank-eyed through her days, a modern-day mystic plugged into a continual bright vision.

In reading a book or watching television, the critics pointed out, the viewer had to exert himself, to participate. But the sensories merely swept over you, vivid, brilliant, insidious, and left behind the damaging schizophrenic impression that dreams were better and more desirable than life. Such an impression could not be allowed, even if it were true. Sensories were dangerous! To be sure, some valid artistic work was done in the sensory form. (One could not discount Verreho, Johnston or Telkin; and Mikkelsen showed promise.) But there was not *much* good work. And weighed against the damaging psychic effects, the lowering of popular taste, the drift toward complete passivity . . .

In another generation, the critics thundered, people will be incapable of reading, thinking or acting!

It was a strong argument. But Blaine, with his 152 years of perspective, remembered much the same sort of arguments hurled at radio, movies, comic books, television and paperbacks. Even the revered novel had once been bitterly chastised for its deviation from the standards of pure poetry. Every innovation seemed culturally destructive; and became, ultimately, a cultural staple, the embodiment of the good old days, the spirit of the Golden Age – to be threatened and finally destroyed by the next innovation.

The sensories, good or bad, were here. Blaine entered the store to partake of them.

After looking over various models he bought a medium-priced Bendix player. Then, with the clerk's aid, he chose three popular recordings and took them into a booth to play. Fastening the electrodes to his forehead, he turned the first one on.

It was a popular historical, a highly romantic rendition of the *Chanson de Roland*, done in a low-intensity non-identification technique that allowed large battle effects and massed movements. The dream began.

. . . and Blaine was in the pass of Roncesvalles on that hot and fateful August morning in 778, standing with Roland's rear guard, watching the main body of Charlemagne's army wind slowly on toward Frankland. The tired veterans slumped in their high-cantled saddles, leather creaked, spurs jingled against bronze stirrup-guards. There was a smell of pine and sweat in the air, a hint of smoke from razed Pampelona, a taste of oiled steel and dry summer grass . . .

Blaine decided to buy it. The next was a high-intensity chase on Venus, in which the viewer identified fully with the hunted but innocent man. The last was a variable-intensity recording of *War and Peace*, with occasional identification sections.

As he paid for his purchases, the clerk winked at him and said, 'Interested in real stuff?'

'Maybe,' Blaine said.

'I got some great party records,' the clerk told him. 'Full identification with switches yet. No? Got a genuine horror piece – man dying in quicksand. The murderers recorded his death for the specialty trade.'

'Perhaps some other time,' Blaine said, moving toward the door.

'And also,' the clerk told him, 'I got a special recording, legitimately made but withheld from the public. A few copies are being bootlegged around. Man reborn from the past. Absolutely genuine.'

'Really?'

'Yes, it's perfectly unique. The emotions come through clear as a bell, sharp as a knife. A collector's item. I predict it'll become a classic.'

'That I'd like to hear,' Blaine said grimly.

He took the unlabeled record back to the booth. In ten

minutes he came out again, somewhat shaken, and purchased it for an exorbitant price. It was like buying a piece of himself.

The clerk and the Rex technicians were right. It was a real collector's item, and would probably become a classic.

Unfortunately, all names had been carefully wiped to prevent the police from tracing its source. He was famous – but in a completely anonymous fashion.

22

Blaine went to his job every day, swept the floor, emptied the wastepaper basket, addressed envelopes, and did a few antique hulls on commission. In the evenings he studied the complex science of 22nd century yacht design. After a while he was given a few small assignments writing publicity releases. He proved talented at this, and was soon promoted to the position of junior yacht designer. He began handling much of the liaison between Jaakobsen Yachts, Ltd., and the various yards building to their design.

He continued to study, but there were few requests for classic hulls. The Jaakobsen brothers handled most of the stock boats, while old Ed Richter, known as the Marvel of Salem, drew up the unusual racers and multi-hulls. Blaine took over publicity and advertising, and had no time for anything else.

It was responsible, necessary work. But it was *not* yacht designing. Irrevocably his life in 2110 was falling into much the same pattern it had assumed in 1958.

Blaine pondered this carefully. On the one hand, he was happy about it. It seemed to settle, once and for all, the conflict between his mind and his borrowed body. Obviously his mind was boss.

On the other hand, the situation didn't speak too well for the quality of that mind. Here was a man who had travelled 152 years into the future, had passed through wonders and horrors, and was working again, with a weary and terrible inevitability, as a junior yacht designer who did everything but design yachts. Was there some fatal flaw in his character, some hidden defect which doomed him to inferiority no matter what his environment?

Moodily he pictured himself flung back a million or so years, to a caveman era. Doubtless, after a period of initial adjustment, he would become a junior designer of dugouts.

Only not *really* a designer. His job would be to count the wampum, check the quality of the tree trunks and contract for outriggers, while some other fellow (probably a Neanderthal genius) did the actual running of the lines.

That was disheartening. But fortunately it was not the only way of viewing the matter. His inevitable return could also be taken as a fine example of internal solidarity, of human steadfastness. He was a man who knew what he was. No matter how his environment changed, he remained true to his function.

Viewed this way, he could be very proud of being eternally and forever a junior yacht designer.

He continued working, fluctuating between these two basic views of himself. Once or twice he saw Marie, but she was usually busy in the high councils of the Rex Corporation. He moved out of his hotel and into a small, tastefully furnished apartment. New York was beginning to feel normal to him.

And, he reminded himself, if he had gained nothing else, he had at least settled his mind-body problem.

But his body was not to be disposed of so lightly. Blaine had overlooked one of the problems likely to exist with the ownership of a strong, handsome, and highly idiosyncratic body such as his.

One day the conflict flared again, more aggravated than ever.

He had left work at the usual time, and was waiting at a corner for his bus. He noticed a woman staring intently at him. She was perhaps twenty-five years old, a buxom, attractive red-head. She was commonly dressed. Her features were bold, yet they had a certain wistful quality.

Blaine realized that he had seen her before but never really noticed her. Now that he thought about it, she had once ridden a helibus with him. Once she had entered a store nearly on his footsteps. And several times she had been passing his building when he left work.

She had been watching him, probably for weeks. But why?

He waited, staring back at her. The woman hesitated a moment, then said, 'Could I talk to you a moment?' Her voice was husky, pleasant, but very nervous. 'Please, Mr. Blaine, it's very important.'

So she knew his name. 'Sure,' Blaine said. 'What is it?'

'Not here. Could we – uh – go somewhere?'

Blaine grinned and shook his head. She seemed harmless enough; but Orc had seemed so, too. Trusting strangers in this world was a good way of losing your mind, your body, or both.

'I don't know you,' Blaine said, 'and I don't know where you learned my name. Whatever you want, you'd better tell me here.'

'I really shouldn't be bothering you,' the woman said in a discouraged voice. 'But I couldn't stop myself, I had to talk to you. I get so lonely sometimes, you know how it is?'

'Lonely? Sure, but why do you want to talk to me?'

She looked at him sadly. 'That's right, you don't know.'

'No, I don't,' Blaine said patiently. 'Why?'

'Can't we go somewhere? I don't like to say it in public like this.'

'You'll have to,' Blaine said, beginning to think that this was a very complicated game indeed.

'Oh, all right,' the woman said, obviously embarrassed. 'I've been following you around for a long time, Mr. Blaine. I found out your name and where you worked. I had to talk to you. It's all on account of that body of yours.'

'What?'

'Your body,' she said, not looking at him. 'You see, it used to be my husband's body before he sold it to the Rex Corporation.'

Blaine's mouth opened, but he could find no adequate words.

23

Blaine had always known that his body had lived its own life in the world before it had been given to him. It had acted, decided, loved, hated, made its own individual imprint upon society and woven its own complex and lasting web of relationships. He could even have assumed that it had been married; most bodies were. But he had preferred not thinking about it. He had let himself believe that everything concerning the previous owner had conveniently disappeared.

His own meeting with Ray Melhill's snatched body should have shown him how naive that attitude was. Now, like it or not, he had to think about it.

They went to Blaine's apartment. The woman, Alice Kranch, sat dejectedly on one side of the couch and accepted a cigarette.

'The way it was,' she said, 'Frank – that was my husband's name, Frank Kranch – he was never satisfied with things, you know? He had a good job as a hunter, but he was never satisfied.'

'A hunter?'

'Yes, he was a spearman in the China game.'

'Hmm,' Blaine said, wondering again what had induced him to go on that hunt. His own needs or Kranch's dormant reflexes? It was annoying to have this mind-body problem come up again just when it had seemed so nicely settled.

'But he wasn't ever satisfied,' Alice Kranch said. 'And it used to make him sore, those fancy rich guys getting themselves killed and going to the hereafter. He always hated the idea of dying like a dog, Frank did.'

'I don't blame him,' Blaine said.

She shrugged her shoulders. 'What can you do? Frank didn't have a chance of making enough money for hereafter insurance. It bothered him. And then he got that big wound on the shoulder that nearly put him under. I suppose you still got the scar?'

Blaine nodded.

'Well, he wasn't ever the same after that. Hunters usually don't think much about death, but Frank started to. He started thinking about it all the time. And then he met this skinny dame from Rex.'

'Marie Thorne?'

'That's the one,' Alice said. 'She was a skinny dame, hard as nails and cold as a fish. I couldn't understand what Frank saw in her. Oh, he played around some, most hunters do. It's on account of the danger. But there's playing around and playing around. He and this fancy Rex dame were thick as thieves. I just couldn't see what Frank saw in her. I mean she was so *skinny*, and so tight-faced. She was pretty in a pinched sort of way, but she looked like she'd wear her clothes to bed, if you know what I mean.'

Blaine nodded, a little painfully. 'Go on.'

'Well, there's no accounting for some tastes, but I thought I knew Frank's. And I guess I did because it turned out he *wasn't* going with her. It was strictly business. He turned up one day and said to me, "Baby, I'm leaving you. I'm taking that big fat trip into the hereafter. There's a nice piece of change in it for you, too." '

Alice sighed and wiped her eyes. 'That big idiot had sold his body! Rex had given him hereafter insurance and an annuity for me, and he was so damned proud of himself! Well, I talked myself blue in the face trying to get him to change his mind. No chance, he was going to eat pie in the sky. To his way of thinking his number was up anyhow, and the next hunt would do him. So off he went. He talked to me once from the Threshold.'

'Is he still there?' Blaine asked, with a prickling sensation at the back of his neck.

'I haven't heard from him in over a year,' Alice said, 'so I guess he's gone on to the hereafter. The bastard!'

She cried for a few moments, then wiped her eyes with a tiny handkerchief and looked mournfully at Blaine. 'I wasn't going to bother you. After all, it was Frank's body to

135

sell and it's yours now. I don't have any claims on it or you. But I got so blue, so lonely.'

'I can imagine,' Blaine murmured, thinking that she was definitely not his type. Objectively speaking, she was pretty enough. Comely but overblown. Her features were well formed, bold, and vividly colored. Her hair, although obviously not a natural red, was shoulder length and of a smooth texture. She was the sort of woman he could picture, hands on hips, arguing with a policeman; hauling in a fishnet; dancing to a flamenco guitar; or herding goats on a mountain path with a full skirt swishing around ample hips, and peasant blouse distended.

But she was not in good taste.

However, he reminded himself, Frank Kranch had found her very much to *his* taste. And he was wearing Kranch's body.

'Most of our friends,' Alice was saying, 'were hunters in the China game. Oh, they dropped around sometimes after Frank left. But you know hunters, they've got just one thing on their minds.'

'Is that a fact?' Blaine asked.

'Yes. And so I moved out of Peking and came back to New York, where I was born. And then one day I saw Frank – I mean you. I could have fainted on the spot. I mean I might have expected it and all, but still it gives you a turn to see your husband's body walking around.'

'I should think so,' Blaine said.

'So I followed you and all. I wasn't ever going to bother you or anything, but it just kept bothering me all the time. And I sort of got to wondering what kind of a man was . . . I mean, Frank was so – well, he and I got along very well, if you know what I mean.'

'Certainly,' Blaine said.

'I'll bet you think I'm terrible!'

'Not at all!' said Blaine. She looked him full in the face, her expression mournful and coquettish. Blaine felt Kranch's old scar throb.

But remember, he told himself, Kranch is gone. Everything is *Blaine* now, Blaine's will, Blaine's way, Blaine's taste . . .

Isn't it?

This problem must be settled, he thought, as he seized the willing Alice and kissed her with an unBlainelike fervor . . .

In the morning Alice made breakfast. Blaine sat, staring out the window, thinking dismal thoughts.

Last night had proven to him conclusively that Kranch was still king of the Kranch-Blaine body-mind. For last night he had been completely unlike himself. He had been fierce, violent, rough, angry and exultant. He had been all the things he had always deplored, had acted with an abandon that must have bordered on madness.

That was not Blaine. That was *Kranch*, the Body Triumphant.

Blaine had always prized delicacy, subtlety, and the grasp of nuance. Too much, perhaps. Yet those had been his virtues, the expressions of his own individual personality. With them, he was Thomas Blaine. Without them he was less than nothing – a shadow cast by the eternally triumphant Kranch.

Gloomily he contemplated the future. He would give up the struggle, become what his body demanded; a fighter, a brawler, a lusty vagabond. Perhaps in time he would grow used to it, even enjoy it . . .

'Breakfast's ready,' Alice announced.

They ate in silence, and Alice mournfully fingered a bruise on her forearm. At last Blaine could stand it no longer.

'Look,' he said, 'I'm sorry.'

'What for?'

'Everything.'

She smiled wanly. 'That's all right. It was my fault, really.'

'I doubt that. Pass the butter please,' Blaine said.

She passed the butter. They ate in silence for a few minutes. Then Alice said, 'I was very, very stupid.'

'Why?'

'I guess I was chasing a dream,' she said. 'I thought I could find Frank all over again. I'm not really that way, Mr. Blaine. But I thought it would be like with Frank.'

'And wasn't it?'

She shook her head. 'No, of course not.'

Blaine put down his coffee cup carefully. He said, 'I suppose Kranch was rougher. I suppose he batted you from wall to wall. I suppose –'

'Oh, no!' she cried. 'Never! Mr. Blaine, Frank was a hunter and he lived a hard life. But with me he was always a perfect gentleman. He had manners, Frank had.'

'He had?'

'He certainly had! Frank was always gentle with me, Mr. Blaine. He was – delicate, if you know what I mean. Nice. Gentle. He was never, *never* rough. To tell the truth, he was the very opposite from you, Mr. Blaine.'

'Uh,' said Blaine.

'Not that there's anything wrong with you,' she said with hasty kindness. 'You *are* a little rough, but I guess it takes all kinds.'

'I guess it does,' Blaine said. 'Yes, I guess it sure does.'

They finished their breakfast in embarrassed silence. Alice, freed of her obsessive dream, left immediately afterwards, with no suggestion that they meet again. Blaine sat in his big chair, staring out the window, thinking.

So he wasn't like Kranch!

The sad truth was, he told himself, he had acted as he *imagined* Kranch would have acted in similar circumstances. It had been pure autosuggestion. Hysterically he had convinced himself that a strong, active, hearty outdoors man would necessarily treat a woman like a wrestling bear.

He had acted out a stereotype. He would feel even sillier if he weren't so relieved at regaining his threatened Blaineism.

He frowned as he remembered Alice's description of Marie: Skinny, hard as nails, cold as fish. *More* stereotyping.

But under the circumstances, he could hardly blame Alice.

24

A few days later, Blaine received word that a communication was waiting for him at the Spiritual Switchboard. He went there after work, and was sent to the booth he had used previously.

Melhill's amplified voice said, 'Hello, Tom.'

'Hello, Ray. I was wondering where you were.'

'I'm still in the Threshold,' Melhill told him, 'but I won't be much longer. I gotta go on and see what the hereafter is like. It pulls at me. But I wanted to talk to you again, Tom. I think you should watch out for Marie Thorne.'

'Now Ray –'

'I mean it. She's been spending all her time at Rex. I don't know what's going on there, they got the conference rooms shielded against psychic invasion. But something's brewing over you, and she's in the middle of it.'

'I'll keep my eyes open,' Blaine said.

'Tom, please take my advice. Get out of New York. Get out fast, while you still have a body and a mind to run it with.'

'I'm staying,' Blaine said.

'You stubborn bastard,' Melhill said, with deep feeling. 'What's the use of having a protective spirit if you don't ever take his advice?'

'I appreciate your help,' Blaine said. 'I really do. But tell me truthfully, how much better off would I be if I ran?'

'You might be able to stay alive a little longer.'

'Only a little? Is it that bad?'

'Bad enough. Tom, remember not to trust *anybody*. I gotta go now.'

'Will I speak to you again, Ray?'

'Maybe,' Melhill said. 'Maybe not. Good luck, kid.'

The interview was ended. Blaine returned to his apartment.

*

The next day was Saturday. Blaine lounged in bed late, made himself breakfast and called Marie. She was out. He decided to spend the day relaxing and playing his sensory recordings.

That afternoon he had two callers.

The first was a gentle, hunchbacked old woman dressed in a dark, severe uniform. Across her army-style cap were the words, 'Old Church.'

'Sir,' she said in a slightly wheezy voice, 'I am soliciting contributions for the Old Church, an organization which seeks to promote faith in these dissolute and Godless times.'

'Sorry,' Blaine said, and started to close the door.

But the old woman must have had many doors closed on her. She wedged herself between door and jamb and continued talking.

'This, young sir, is the age of the Babylonian Beast, and the time of the soul's destruction. This is Satan's age, and the time of his seeming triumph. But be not deceived! The Lord Almighty has allowed this to come about for a trial and a testing, and a winnowing of grain from chaff. Beware the temptation! Beware the path of evil which lies splendid and glittering before you!'

Blaine gave her a dollar just to shut her up. The old woman thanked him but continued talking.

'Beware, young sir, that ultimate lure of Satan – the false heaven which men call the hereafter! For what better snare could Satan the Deceiver devise for the world of men than this, his greatest illusion! The illusion that hell is heaven! And men are deceived by the cunning deceit, and willingly go down into it!'

'Thank you,' Blaine said, trying to shut the door.

'Remember my words!' the old woman cried, fixing him with a glassy blue eye. 'The hereafter is evil! Beware the prophets of the hellish afterlife!'

'Thank you!' Blaine cried, and managed to close the door.

He relaxed in his armchair again and turned on the player. For nearly an hour he was absorbed in *Flight on Venus*. Then there was a knock on his door.

Blaine opened it, and saw a short, well-dressed, chubby-faced, earnest-looking young man.

'Mr. Thomas Blaine?' the man asked.

'That's me.'

'Mr. Blaine, I am Charles Farrell, from the Hereafter Corporation. Might I speak to you? If it is inconvenient now, perhaps we could make an appointment for some other –'

'Come in,' Blaine said, opening the door wide for the prophet of the hellish afterlife.

Farrell was a mild, businesslike, soft-spoken prophet. His first move was to give Blaine a letter written on Hereafter, Inc. stationery, stating that Charles Farrell was a fully authorized representative of the Hereafter Corporation. Included in the letter was a meticulous description of Farrell, his signature, three stamped photographs and a set of fingerprints.

'And here are my identity proofs,' Farrell said, opening his wallet and showing his heli license, library card, voter's registration certificate and government clearance card. On a separate piece of treated paper Farrell impressed the fingerprints of his right hand and gave them to Blaine for comparison with those on the letter.

'Is all this necessary?' Blaine asked.

'Absolutely,' Farrell told him. 'We've had some unhappy occurrences in the past. Unscrupulous operators frequently try to pass themselves off as Hereafter representatives among the gullible and the poor. They offer salvation at a cut rate, take what they can get and skip town. Too many people have been cheated out of everything they own, and get nothing in return. For the illegal operators, even when they represent some little fly-by-night salvation company, have none of the expensive equipment and trained technicians that are needed for this sort of thing.'

'I didn't know,' Blaine said. 'Won't you sit down?'

Farrell took a chair. 'The Better Business Bureaus are trying to do something about it. But the fly-by-nights move too fast to be easily caught. Only Hereafter, Inc. and two other companies with government-approved techniques are able to deliver what they promise – a life after death.'

'What about the various mental disciplines?' Blaine asked.

'I was purposely excluding them,' Farrell said. 'They're a completely different category. If you have the patience and determination necessary for twenty years or so of concentrated study, more power to you. If you don't, then you need scientific aid and implementation. And that's where we come in.'

'I'd like to hear about it,' Blaine said.

Mr. Farrell settled himself more comfortably in his chair. 'If you're like most people, you probably want to know what is life? What is death? What is a mind? Where is the interaction point between mind and body? Is the mind also soul? Is the soul also mind? Are they independent of each other, or interdependent, or intermixed? Or is there any such thing as a soul?' Farrell smiled. 'Are those some of the questions you want me to answer?'

Blaine nodded. Farrell said, 'Well, I can't. We simply don't know, haven't the slightest idea. As far as we're concerned those are religiophilosophical questions which Hereafter, Inc. has no intention of even *trying* to answer. We're interested in results, not speculation. Our orientation is medical. Our approach is pragmatic. We don't care how or why we get our results, or how strange they seem. *Do they work?* That's the only question we ask, and that's our basic position.'

'I think you've made it clear,' Blaine said.

'It's important for me to do so at the start. So let me make one more thing clear. Don't make the mistake of thinking that we are offering heaven.'

'No?'

'Not at all! Heaven is a religious concept, and we have nothing to do with religion. Our hereafter is a survival of the *mind* after the body's death. That's all. We don't claim the hereafter is heaven any more than early scientists claimed that the bones of the first cavemen were the remains of Adam and Eve.'

142

'An old woman called here earlier,' Blaine said. 'She told me that the hereafter is hell.'

'She's a fanatic,' Farrell said, grinning. 'She follows me around. And for all I know, she's perfectly right.'

'What *do* you know about the hereafter?'

'Not very much,' Farrell told him. 'All we know for sure is this: After the body's death, the mind moves to a region we call the Threshold, which exists between Earth and the hereafter. It is, we believe, a sort of preparatory state to the hereafter itself. Once the mind is there, it can move at will into the hereafter.'

'But what is the hereafter like?'

'We don't know. We're fairly sure it's nonphysical. Past that, everything is conjecture. Some think that the mind is the essence of the body, and therefore the essences of a man's worldly goods can be brought into the hereafter with him. It could be so. Others disagree. Some feel that the hereafter is a place where souls await their turn for rebirth on other planets as part of a vast reincarnation cycle. Perhaps that's true, too. Some feel that the hereafter is only the first stage of post-Earth existence, and that there are six others, increasingly difficult to attain, culminating in a sort of nirvana. Could be. It's been said that the hereafter is a vast, misty region where you wander alone, forever searching, never finding. I've read theories that prove people must be grouped in the hereafter according to family; others say you're grouped there according to race, or religion, or skin coloration, or social position. Some people, as you've observed, say it's hell itself you're entering. There are advocates of a theory of illusion, who claim that the mind vanishes completely when it leaves the Threshold. And there are people who accuse us at the corporation of faking all our effects. A recent learned work states that you'll find whatever you want in the hereafter – heaven, paradise, valhalla, green pastures, take your choice. A claim is made that the old gods rule in the hereafter – the gods of Haiti, Scandinavia or the Belgian Congo, depending on whose theory you're following. Naturally a countertheory shows that there can't be any gods at all. I've seen an English book proving that English spirits rule the hereafter, and a Russian book claiming that the Russians rule, and several American books that prove the Americans rule. A book came out last year stating that the government of the hereafter is anarchy. A leading philosopher insists that competition is a law of nature, and must be so in the hereafter, too. And so on. You can take your pick of any of those theories, Mr. Blaine, or you can make up one of your own.'

'What do you think?' Blaine asked.

'Me? I'm keeping an open mind,' Farrell said. 'When the time comes, I'll go there and find out.'

'That's good enough for me,' Blaine said. 'Unfortunately, I won't have a chance. I don't have the kind of money you people charge.'

'I know,' Farrell said. 'I checked into your finances before I called.'

'Then why —'

'Every year,' Farrell said, 'a number of free hereafter grants are made, some by philanthropists, some by corporations and trusts, a few on a lottery basis. I am happy to say, Mr. Blaine, that you have been selected for one of these grants.'

'Me?'

'Let me offer my congratulations,' Farrell said. 'You're a very lucky man.'

'But who gave me the grant?'

'The Main-Farbenger Textile Corporation.'

'I never heard of them.'

'Well, they heard of you. The grant is in recognition of your trip here from the year 1958. Do you accept it?'

Blaine stared hard at the hereafter representative. Farrell seemed genuine enough; anyhow, his story could be checked at the Hereafter Building. Blaine had his suspicions of the splendid gift thrust so unexpectedly into his hands. But the thought of an assured life after death outweighed any possible doubts, thrust aside any possible fears. Caution was all very well; but not when the gates of the hereafter were opening before you.

'What do I have to do?' he asked.

'Simply accompany me to the Hereafter Building,' Farrell said. 'We can have the necessary work done in a few hours.'

Survival! Life after death!

'All right,' Blaine said. 'I accept the grant. Let's go!'

They left Blaine's apartment at once.

25

A helicab brought them directly to the Hereafter Building. Farrell led the way to the Admissions Office, and gave a photostatic copy of Blaine's grant to the woman in charge. Blaine made a set of fingerprints, and produced his Hunter's License for further identity. The woman checked all the data carefully against her master list of acceptances. Finally she was satisfied with its validity, and signed the admission papers.

Farrell then took Blaine to the Testing Room, wished him luck, and left him.

In the Testing Room, a squad of young technicians took over and ran Blaine through a gamut of examinations. Banks of calculators clicked and rattled, and spewed forth yards of papers and showers of punched cards. Ominous machines bubbled and squeaked at him, glared with giant red eyes, winked and turned amber. Automatic pens squiggled across pieces of graph paper. And through it all, the technicians kept up a lively shop talk.

'Interesting beta reaction. Think we can fair that curve?'

'Sure, sure, just lower his drive coefficient.'

'Hate to do that. It weakens the web.'

'You don't have to weaken it *that* much. He'll still take the trauma.'

'Maybe . . . What about this Henliger factor? It's off.'

'That's because he's in a host body. It'll come around.'

'That one didn't last week. The guy went up like a rocket.'

'He was a little unstable to begin with.'

Blaine said, 'Hey! Is there any chance of this not working?'

The technicians turned as though seeing him for the first time.

'Every case is different, pal,' a technician told him.

'Each one has to be worked out on an individual basis.'

'It's just problems, problems all the time.'

Blaine said, 'I thought the treatment was all worked out. I heard it was infallible.'

'Sure, that's what they tell the customers,' one of the technicians said scornfully.

'That's advertising crap.'

'Things go wrong here every day. We still got a long way to go.'

Blaine said, 'But can you tell if the treatment takes?'

'Of course. If it takes, you're still alive.'

'If it doesn't you never walk out of here.'

'It *usually* takes,' a technician said consolingly. 'On everybody but a K3.'

'It's that damned K3 factor that throws us. Come on, Jamieson, is he a K3 or not?'

'I'm not sure,' Jamieson said, hunched over a flashing instrument. 'The testing machine is all screwed up again.'

Blaine said, 'What is a K3?'

'I wish *we* knew,' Jamieson said moodily. 'All we know for certain, guys with a K3 factor can't survive after death.'

'Not under any circumstances.'

'Old Fitzroy thinks it's a built-in limiting factor that nature included so the species wouldn't run wild.'

'But K3s don't transmit the factor to their children.'

'There's still a chance it lies dormant and skips a few generations.'

'Am I a K3?' Blaine asked, trying to keep his voice steady.

'Probably not,' Jamieson said easily. 'It's sort of rare. Let me check.'

Blaine waited while the technicians went over their data, and Jamieson tried to determine from his faulty machine whether or not Blaine had a K3 factor.

After a while, Jamieson looked up. 'Well, I guess he's not K3. Though who knows, really? Anyhow, let's get on with it.'

'What comes next?' Blaine asked.

A hypodermic bit deeply into his arm.

'Don't worry,' a technician told him, 'everything's going to be just fine.'

'Are you *sure* I'm not K3?' Blaine asked. The technician nodded in a perfunctory manner. Blaine wanted to ask more questions, but a wave of dizziness overcame him. The technicians were lifting him, putting him on a white operating table.

When he recovered consciousness he was lying on a comfortable couch listening to soothing music. A nurse handed him a glass of sherry, and Mr. Farrell was standing by, beaming.

'Feel OK?' Farrell asked. 'You should. Everything went off perfectly.'

'It did?'

'No possibility of error. Mr. Blaine, the hereafter is yours.'

Blaine finished his sherry and stood up, a little shakily. 'Life after death is mine? Whenever I die? Whatever I die of?'

'That's right. No matter how or when you die, your mind will survive after death. How do you feel?'

'I don't know,' Blaine said.

It was only half an hour later, as he was returning to his apartment, that he began to react.

The hereafter was his!

He was filled with a sudden wild elation. Nothing mattered now, nothing whatsoever! He was immortal! He could be killed on the spot and yet live on!

He felt superbly drunk. Gaily he contemplated throwing himself under the wheels of a passing truck. What did it matter? Nothing could really hurt him! He could berserk now, slash merrily through the crowds. Why not? The only thing the flathats could really kill was his body!

The feeling was indescribable. Now, for the first time, Blaine realized what men had lived with before the discovery of the scientific hereafter. He remembered the heavy, sodden, constant, unconscious fear of death that subtly weighed every action and permeated every movement. The ancient enemy death, the shadow that

148

crept down the corridors of a man's mind like some grisly tapeworm, the ghost that haunted nights and days, the croucher behind corners, the shape behind doors, the unseen guest at every banquet, the unidentified figure in every landscape, always present, always waiting –

No more.

For now a tremendous weight had been lifted from his mind. The fear of death was gone, intoxicatingly gone, and he felt light as air. Death, that ancient enemy, was defeated!

He returned to his apartment in a state of high euphoria. The telephone was ringing as he unlocked the door.

'Blaine speaking!'

'Tom!' It was Marie Thorne. 'Where have you been? I've been trying to reach you all afternoon.'

'I've been out, darling,' Blaine said. 'Where in the hell have you been?'

'At Rex,' she said. 'I've been trying to find out what they're up to. Now listen carefully, I have some important news for you.'

'I've got some news for you, sweetheart,' Blaine said.

'Listen to me! A man will call at your apartment today. He'll be a salesman from Hereafter, Inc., and he will offer you free hereafter insurance. Don't take it.'

'Why not? Is he a fake?'

'No, he's perfectly genuine, and so is the offer. But you mustn't take it.'

'I already did,' Blaine said.

'You what?'

'He was here a few hours ago. I accepted it.'

'Have they treated you yet?'

'Yes. Was that a fake?'

'No,' Marie said, 'of course it wasn't. Oh Tom, when will you learn not to accept gifts from strangers? There was time for hereafter insurance later . . . Oh, Tom!'

'What's wrong?' Blaine asked. 'It was a grant from the Main-Farbenger Textile Corporation.'

'They are owned completely by the Rex Corporation,' Marie told him.

'Oh . . . But so what?'

'Tom, the directors of Rex gave you that grant. They used Main-Farbenger as a front, but *Rex* gave you that grant! Can't you see what it means?'

'No. Will you please stop screaming and explain?'

'Tom, it's the Permitted Murder section of the Suicide Act. They're going to invoke it.'

'What are you talking about?'

'I'm talking about the section of the Suicide Act that makes host-taking legal. Rex has guaranteed the survival of your mind after death, you've accepted it. Now they can legally take your body for any purpose they desire. They own it. They can *kill* your body, Tom!'

'Kill me?'

'Yes. And of course they're going to. The government is planning action against them for illegally transporting you from the past. If you're not around, there's no case. Now listen. You *must* get out of New York, then out of the country. Maybe they'll leave you alone then. I'll help. I think that you should –'

The telephone went dead.

Blaine clicked the receiver several times, but got no dial tone. Apparently the line had been cut.

The elation he had been filled with a few seconds ago drained out of him. The intoxicating sense of freedom from death vanished. How could he have contemplated berserking? He wanted to *live*. He wanted to live in the flesh, upon the Earth he knew and loved. Spiritual existence was fine, but he didn't want it yet. Not for a long time. He wanted to live among solid objects, breathe air, eat bread and drink water, feel flesh surround him, touch other flesh.

When would they try to kill him? Any time at all. His apartment was like a trap. Quickly Blaine scooped all his money into a pocket and hurried to the door. He opened it, and looked up and down the hall. It was empty.

He hurried out, ran down the corridor, and stopped.

A man had just come around the corner. The man was standing in the center of the hall. He was carrying a large projector, which was levelled at Blaine's stomach.

The man was Sammy Jones.

'Ah, Tom, Tom,' Jones sighed. 'Believe me, I'm damned sorry it's you. But business is business.'

Blaine stood, frozen, as the projector lifted to level on his chest.

'Why you?' Blaine managed to ask.

'Who else?' Sammy Jones said. 'Aren't I the best hunter in the Western Hemisphere, and probably Europe, too? Rex hired every one of us in the New York area. But with beam and projectile weapons this time. I'm sorry it's you, Tom.'

'But I'm a hunter, too,' Blaine said.

'You won't be the first that got gunned. It's the breaks of the game, lad. Don't flinch. I'll make it quick and clean.'

'I don't want to die!' Blaine gasped.

'Why not?' Jones asked. 'You've got your hereafter insurance.'

'I was tricked! I want to live! Sammy, don't do it!'

Sammy Jones' face hardened. He took careful aim, then lowered the gun.

'I'm growing too soft-hearted for this game,' Jones said. 'All right, Tom, start moving. I guess every Quarry should have a little head start. Makes it more sporting. But I'm only giving you a little.'

'Thanks, Sammy,' Blaine said, and hurried down the hall.

'But Tom – watch your step if you really want to live. I'm telling you, there's more hunters than citizens in New York right now. And every means of transportation is guarded.'

'Thanks,' Blaine called, as he hurried down the stairs.

He was in the street, but he didn't know where to go. Still, he had no time for indecision. It was late afternoon, hours before darkness could help him. He picked a direction and began walking.

Almost instinctively, his steps were leading him toward the slums of the city.

26

He walked past the rickety tenements and ancient apartment houses, past the cheap saloons and night clubs, hands thrust in his pockets, trying to think. He would have to come up with a plan. The hunters would get him in the next hour or two if he couldn't work out some plan, some way of getting out of New York.

Jones had told him that the transportation services were being watched. What hope had he, then? He was unarmed, defenceless –'

Well, perhaps he could change that. With a gun in his hand, things would be a little different. In fact, things might be very different indeed. As Hull had pointed out, a hunter could legally shoot a Quarry; but if a Quarry shot a hunter he was liable for arrest and severe penalties.

If he did shoot a hunter, the police would have to arrest him! It would all get very involved, but it would save him from the immediate danger.

He walked until he came to a pawnshop. In the window was a glittering array of projectile and beam weapons, hunting rifles, knives and machetes. Blaine went in.

'I want a gun,' he said to the moustached man behind the counter.

'A gun. So. And what kind of a gun?' the man asked.

'Have you got any beamers?'

The man nodded and went to a drawer. He took out a gleaming handgun with a bright copper finish.

'Now this,' he said, 'is a special buy. It's a genuine Sailes-Byrn needlebeam, used for hunting big Venusian game. At five hundred yards you can cut through anything that walks, crawls or flies. On the side is the aperture selector. You can fan wide for close-range work, or extend to a needle point for distance shooting.'

'Fine, fine,' Blaine said, pulling bills from his pocket.

'This button here,' the pawnbroker said, 'controls length of blast. Set as is, you get a standard fractional jolt. One click extends time to a quarter second. Put it on automatic and it'll cut like a scythe. It has a power supply of over four hours, and there's more than three hours still left in the original pack. What's more, you can use this weapon in your home workshop. With a special mounting and a baffle to cut down the power, you can slice plastic with this better than with a saw. A different baffle converts it into a blowtorch. The baffles can be purchased –'

'I'll buy it,' Blaine broke in.

The pawnbroker nodded. 'May I see your permit, please?'

Blaine took out his Hunter's License and showed it to the man. The pawnbroker nodded, and, with maddening slowness, filled out a receipt.

'Shall I wrap it?'

'Don't bother. I'll take it as it is.'

The pawnbroker said, 'That'll be seventy-five dollars.' As Blaine pushed the money across the counter, the pawnbroker consulted a list on the wall behind him.

'Hold it!' he said suddenly.

'Eh?'

'I can't sell you that weapon.'

'Why not?' Blaine asked. 'You saw my Hunter's License.'

'But you didn't tell me you were a registered Quarry. You know a Quarry can't have weapons. Your name was flashed here half an hour ago. You can't buy a legal weapon anywhere in New York, Mr. Blaine.'

The pawnbroker pushed the bills back across the counter. Blaine grabbed for the needle-beam. The pawnbroker scooped it up first and levelled it at him.

'I ought to save them the trouble,' he said. 'You've got your damned hereafter. What else do you want?'

Blaine stood perfectly still. The pawnbroker lowered the gun.

'But that's not my job,' he said. 'The hunters will get you soon enough.'

He reached under the counter and pressed a button. Blaine turned and ran out of the store. It was growing dark. But his location had been revealed. The hunters would be closing in now.

He thought he heard someone calling his name. He pushed through the crowds, not looking back, trying to think of something to do. He couldn't die like this, could he? He couldn't have come 152 years through time to be shot before a million people! It just wasn't fair!

He noticed a man following close behind him, grinning. It was Theseus, gun out, waiting for a clear shot.

Blaine put on a burst of speed, dodged through the crowds and turned quickly into a side street. He sprinted down it, then came to a sudden stop.

At the far end of the street, silhouetted against the light, a man was standing. The man had one hand on his hip, the other raised in a shooting position. Blaine hesitated, and glanced back at Theseus.

The little hunter fired, scorching Blaine's sleeve. Blaine ran toward an open door, which was suddenly slammed in his face. A second shot charred his coat.

With dreamlike clarity he watched the hunters advance, Theseus close behind him, the other hunter in the distance, blocking the way out. Blaine ran on leaden feet, toward the more distant man, over manhole covers and subway gratings, past shuttered stores and locked buildings.

'Back off, Theseus!' the hunter called. 'I got him!'

'Take him, Hendrick!' Theseus called back, and flattened himself against a wall, out of the way of the blast.

The gunman, fifty feet away, took aim and fired. Blaine fell flat and the beam missed him. He rolled, trying to make the inadequate shelter of a doorway. The beam probed after him, scoring the concrete and turning the puddles of sewer water into steam.

Then a subway grating gave way beneath him.

As he fell, he knew that the grating must have been weakened by the lancing beam. Blind luck! But he had to land on his feet. He had to stay conscious, drag himself away from the opening, use his luck. If he went

154

unconscious, his body would be lying in full view of the opening, an easy target for hunters standing on the edge.

He tried to twist in mid-air, too late. He landed heavily on his shoulders, and his head slammed against an iron stanchion. But the need to stay conscious was so great that he pulled himself to his feet.

He had to drag himself out of the way, deep into the subway passage, far enough so they couldn't find him.

But even the first step was too much. Sickeningly, his legs buckled under him. He fell on his face, rolled over and stared at the gaping hole above him.

Then he passed out.

PART FOUR

PART FOUR

27

When he revived, Blaine decided that he didn't like the hereafter. It was dark, lumpy, and it smelled of oil and slime. Also, his head ached, and his back felt as though it had been broken in three places.

Could a spirit ache? Blaine moved, and discovered that he still had a body. As a matter of fact, he felt all body. Apparently he wasn't in the hereafter.

'Just rest a minute,' a voice said.

'Who is it?' Blaine asked into the impenetrable darkness.

'Smith.'

'Oh. You.' Blaine sat up and held his throbbing head. 'How did you do it, Smith?'

'I nearly didn't,' the zombie told him. 'As soon as you were declared Quarry, I came for you. Some of my friends down here volunteered to help, but you were moving too fast. I shouted to you when you came out of the pawnshop.'

'I thought I heard a voice,' Blaine said.

'If you'd turned around, we could have taken you in there and then. But you didn't so we followed. A few times we opened subway grates and manhole covers for you, but it was hard to gauge it right. We were a little late each time.'

'But not the last time,' Blaine said.

'At last I had to open a grate right under you. I'm sorry you hit your head.'

'Where am I?'

'I pulled you out of the main line,' Smith said. 'You're in a side passageway. The hunters can't find you here.'

Blaine once again could find no adequate words for thanking Smith. And Smith once again wanted no thanks.

'I'm not doing it for you, Blaine. It's for me. I need you.'

'Have you found out why yet?'

'Not yet,' Smith said.

Blaine's eyes, adjusting to the gloom, could make out the

outline of the zombie's head and shoulders. 'What now?' he asked.

'Now you're safe. We can bring you underground as far as New Jersey. From there you're on your own. But I don't think you should have much trouble then.'

'What are we waiting for now?'

'Mr. Kean. I need his permission to take you through the passageways.'

They waited. In a few minutes, Blaine was able to make out Mr. Kean's thin shape, leaning on the big Negro's arm, coming toward him.

'I'm sorry about your troubles,' Kean said, sitting down beside Blaine. 'It's a great pity.'

'Mr. Kean,' Smith said, 'if I could just be allowed to take him through the old Holland Tunnel, into New Jersey —'

'I'm truly sorry,' Kean said, 'but I cannot allow it.'

Blaine looked around and saw that he was surrounded by a dozen ragged zombies.

'I've spoken to the hunters,' Kean said, 'and I have given them my guarantee that you will be back on the surface streets within half an hour. You must leave now, Blaine.'

'But why?'

'We simply can't afford to help you,' Kean said. 'I was taking an unusual risk the first time, allowing you to defile Reilly's tomb. But I did it for Smith, because his destiny seems linked with yours in some way. And Smith is one of my people. But this is too much. You know we are allowed to live underground upon sufferance only.'

'I know,' Blaine said.

'Smith should have considered the consequences. When he opened that grating for you, the hunters poured in. They didn't find you, but they knew you were down here somewhere. So they searched, Blaine, they searched! Dozens of them, exploring our passageways, pushing our people around, threatening, shouting, talking on their little radios. Reporters came too, and even idle spectators. Some of the younger hunters became nervous and started shooting at the zombies.'

'I'm very sorry about that,' Blaine said.

'It wasn't your fault. But Smith should have known better. The world of the underground is not a sovereign kingdom. We exist on sufferance only, on a toleration which might be wiped out at any time. So I spoke to the hunters and the reporters.'

'What did you tell them?' Blaine asked.

'I told them that a faulty grate had given way beneath you. I said you had fallen in by accident and had crawled into hiding. I assured them that no zombie had been involved in this; that we found you and would place you back on the surface streets within half an hour. They accepted my word and left. I wish I could have done otherwise.'

'I don't blame you,' Blaine said, getting slowly to his feet.

'I didn't specify where you would emerge,' Kean said. 'At the very least, you'll have a better chance than before. I wish I could do more, but I cannot allow the underground to become a stage for hunts. We must stay neutral, annoy no one, frighten no one. Only in that way will we survive until an age of understanding is reached.'

'Where am I going to come out?' Blaine asked.

'I have chosen an unused subway exit at West 79th Street,' Mr. Kean said. 'You should have a good chance from there. And I have done one more thing which I probably shouldn't have done.'

'What's that?'

'I have contacted a friend of yours, who will be waiting at the exit. But please don't tell anyone about it. Let's hurry now!'

Mr. Kean led the procession through the winding underground maze, and Blaine brought up the rear, his headache slowly subsiding. Soon they stopped beside a concrete staircase.

'Here is the exit,' Kean said. 'Good luck, Blaine.'

'Thanks,' Blaine said. 'And Smith – thanks.'

'I've tried my best for you,' Smith said. 'If you die, I'll probably die. If you live, I'll keep on trying to remember.'

'And if you do remember?'

'Then I'll come and visit you,' Smith said.

Blaine nodded and walked up the staircase.

It was full night outside, and 79th Street seemed deserted. Blaine stood beside the exit, looking around, wondering what to do.

'Blaine!'

Someone was calling him. But it was not Marie, as he had expected. It was a man's voice, someone he knew – Sammy Jones, perhaps, or Theseus.

He turned quickly back to the subway exit. It was closed and fastened securely.

28

'Tom, Tom, it's me!'

'Ray?'

'Of course! Keep your voice down. There's hunters not far away. Wait now.'

Blaine waited, crouched beside the barred subway exit, peering around. He could see no sign of Melhill. There was no ectoplasmic vapor, nothing except a whispering voice.

'OK,' Melhill said. 'Walk west now. Quickly.'

Blaine walked, sensing Melhill's invisible presence hovering near him. He said, 'Ray, how come?'

'It's about time I was some help,' Melhill said. 'That old Kean contacted your girl friend and she got in touch with me through the Spiritual Switchboard. Wait! Stop right here.'

Blaine ducked back against the corner of a building. A heli cruised slowly by at housetop level.

'Hunters,' Melhill said. 'There's a field day on you, kid. Reward posted. Even a reward for information leading to. Tom, I told Marie I'd try to help. Don't know how long I can. Drains me. It's hereafter for me after this.'

'Ray, I don't know how –'

'Cut it out. Look Tom, I can't talk much. Marie has fixed a deal with some friends of hers. They've got a plan, if I can get you to them. Stop!'

Blaine stopped and found shelter behind a mail-box. Long seconds passed. Then three hunters hurried by, sidearms ready. After they turned a corner, Blaine was able to start walking again.

'Some eyes you have,' he said to Melhill.

'The vision's pretty good up here,' Melhill said. 'Cross this street fast.'

Blaine sprinted across. For the next fifteen minutes, at Melhill's instructions, he wound in and out of streets, advancing and retreating across the battleground of the city.

'This is it,' Melhill said at last. 'That door over there, number 341. You made it! I'll see you, Tom. Watch –'

At that moment, two men rounded a corner, stopped, and stared hard at Blaine. One said, 'Hey, that's the guy!'

'What guy?'

'The guy they got the reward out for. Hey *you*!'

They ran forward. Blaine, his fists swinging, quickly chopped the first man into unconsciousness. He whirled, looking for the second, but Melhill had the situation well in control.

The second man had his hands over his head, trying to guard himself. A garbage can cover, levitating mysteriously, was clanging angrily around his ears. Blaine stepped forward and finished the job.

'Damn good,' Melhill said, his voice very weak. 'Always wanted to try ghosting. But it drains . . . Luck, Tom!'

'Ray!' Blaine waited, but there was no answer, and the sense of Melhill's presence was gone.

Blaine waited no longer. He went to number 341, opened the door and stepped in.

He was in a narrow hallway. At the end of it was a door. Blaine knocked.

'Come in,' he was told.

He opened the door and walked into a small, dingy, heavily curtained room.

Blaine had thought he was proof against any further surprises. But it gave him a start all the same to see, grinning at him, Carl Orc, the body snatcher. And sitting beside him, also grinning, was Joe, the little Transplant peddler.

29

Blaine made an automatic move backwards toward the door, but Orc beckoned him in. The body snatcher was unchanged, still very tall and thin, his tanned face long and mournful, his eyes narrow, direct and honest. His clothes still hung awkwardly on him, as though he were more used to levis than to tailored slacks.

'We were expecting you,' Orc said. 'Of course you remember Joe.'

Blaine nodded, remembering very well the furtive-eyed little man who had distracted his attention so that Orc could drug his drink.

'Happy to see you again,' Joe said.

'I'll bet,' Blaine said, not moving from the door.

'Come in and sit down,' Orc said. 'We ain't planning to eat you, Tom. Truly not. Let's let bygones be bygones.'

'You tried to kill me.'

'That was business,' Orc said in his straightforward fashion. 'We're on the same side now.'

'How can I be sure of that?'

'No man,' Orc stated, 'has ever questioned my honesty. Not when I'm really being honest, which I am now. Miss Thorne hired us to get you safe out of the country, and we intend to do same. Sit down and let's discuss it. Are you hungry?'

Reluctantly Blaine sat down. There were sandwiches on a table, and a bottle of red wine. He realized that he hadn't eaten all day. He started wolfing down sandwiches while Orc lighted a thin brown cigar, and Joe appeared to be dozing.

'You know,' Orc said, exhaling blue smoke, 'I very nearly didn't take this job. Not that the money wasn't right; I think Miss Thorne was more than generous. But Tom, this is one of the biggest manhunts our fair city's seen for a while. Ever see anything like it, Joe?'

'Never,' Joe said, shaking his head rapidly. 'Town's covered like flypaper.'

'Rex really wants you,' Orc said. 'They've set their little hearts on nailing your corpus where they can see it. Makes a man nervous, bucking an organization that size. But it's a challenge, a real man-sized challenge.'

'Carl likes a big challenge,' Joe said.

'I admit that,' Orc said. 'Particularly if there's a big profit to be made from it.'

'But where can I go?' Blaine asked. 'Where won't Rex find me?'

'Just about nowhere,' Orc said sadly.

'Off the Earth? Mars? Venus?'

'Even worse. The planets have just a few towns and small cities. Everybody knows everybody else. The news would be all over in a week. Also, you wouldn't fit in. Aside from the Chinese on Mars, the planets are still populated mostly with scientific types and their families, and a few youth-training programs. You wouldn't like it.'

'Where, then?'

'That's what I asked Miss Thorne,' Orc said. 'We discussed several possibilities. First, there's a zombie-making operation. I could perform it. Rex would never search for you underground.'

'I'd rather die,' Blaine said.

'I would too,' Orc agreed. 'So we ruled it out. We thought about finding you a little farm in the Atlantic Abyss. Pretty lonely territory out there. But it takes a special mentality to live undersea and like it, and we didn't figure you had it. You'd probably crack up. So, after due consideration, we decided the best place for you was in the Marquesas.'

'The what?'

'The Marquesas. They're a scattered group of small islands, originally Polynesian, out towards the middle of the Pacific Ocean. They're not too far from Tahiti.'

'The South Seas,' Blaine said.

'Right. We figured you should feel more at home there than anywhere else on Earth. It's just like the 20th century,

166

I'm told. And even more important, Rex might leave you alone.'

'Why would they?'

'For obvious reasons, Tom. Why do they want to kill you in the first place? Because they snatched you illegally from the past and they're worried about what the government's going to do about it. But your going to the Marquesas removes you from the jurisdiction of the U.S. government. Without you, there's no case. And your going so far is a sign to Rex of your good faith. It certainly isn't the act of a man who's going to blab to Uncle Sam. Also, the Marquesas are an independent little nation since the French gave them up, so Rex would have to get special permission to hunt you there. On the whole, it *should* be just too much trouble for everyone concerned. The U.S. government will undoubtedly drop the matter, and I think Rex will leave you alone.'

'Is that certain?' Blaine asked.

'Of course not. It's conjecture. But it's reasonable.'

'Couldn't we make a deal with Rex beforehand?'

Orc shook his head. 'In order to bargain, Tom, you have to have something to bargain with. As long as you're in New York, it's easier and safer for them to kill you.'

'I guess you're right,' Blaine said. 'How are you going to get me out?'

Orc and Joe looked at each other uncomfortably. Orc said, 'Well, that was our big problem. There just didn't seem to be any way of getting you out alive.'

'Heli or jet?'

'They have to stop at the air tolls, and hunters are waiting at all of them. Surface vehicle is equally out of the question.'

'Disguise?'

'Maybe it would have worked during the first hour of the hunt. Now it's impossible, even if we could get you a complete plastic surgery job. By now the hunters are equipped with identity scanners. They'd see through you in a moment.'

'Then there's no way out?' Blaine asked.

Orc and Joe exchanged another uneasy glance. 'There is,' Orc said. 'Just one way. But you probably won't like it.'

167

'I like to stay alive. What is it?'

Orc paused and lighted another cigar. 'We plan to quick-freeze you to near absolute zero, like for spaceship travel. Then we'll ship your carcass out in a crate of frozen beef. Your body will be in the center of the load, so most likely it won't be detected.'

'Sounds risky,' Blaine said.

'Not too risky,' Orc said.

Blaine frowned, sensing something wrong. 'I'll be unconscious through it, won't I?'

After a long pause, Orc said, 'No.'

'I won't?'

'It can't be done that way,' Orc told him. 'The fact is, you and your body will have to separate. That's the part I'm afraid you won't like.'

'What in hell are you talking about?' Blaine asked, getting to his feet.

'Take it easy,' Orc said. 'Sit down, smoke a cigarette, have some more wine. It's like this, Tom. We can't ship out a quick-frozen body with a mind in it. The hunters are waiting for something like that. Can you imagine what happens when they run a quick scan over that shipment of beef and detect a dormant mind in it? Up goes the kite! *Adieu la musique!* I'm not trying to con you, Tom. It just can't be done like that.'

'Then what happens to my mind?' Blaine asked, sitting down again.

'That,' Orc said, 'is where Joe comes in. Tell him, Joe.'

Joe nodded rapidly. 'Transplant, my friend, is the answer.'

'Transplant?'

'I told you about it,' Joe said, 'on that inauspicious evening when we first met. Remember? Transplant, the great pastime, the game any number can play, the jolt for jaded minds, the tonic for tired bodies. We've got a worldwide network of Transplantees, Mr. Blaine. Folks who like to switch around, men and women who get tired of wearing the same old body. We're going to key you into the organization.'

'You're going to ship my *mind* across the country?' Blaine asked.

'That's it! From body to body,' Joe told him. 'Believe me, it's instructive as well as entertaining.'

Blaine got to his feet so quickly that he knocked over his chair. 'Like hell!' he said. 'I told you then and I'm telling you now, I'm not playing your lousy little game. I'll take my chances on the street.'

He started toward the door.

Joe said, 'I know it's a little frightening, but –'

'No!'

Orc shouted, 'Damn it, Blaine, will you at least let the man speak?'

'All right,' Blaine said. 'Speak.'

Joe poured himself half a glass of wine and threw it down. He said, 'Mr. Blaine, it's going to be difficult explaining this to you, a guy from the past. But try to understand what I'm saying.'

Blaine nodded warily.

'Now then. Transplant is used as a sex game these days, and that's how I peddle it. Why? Because people are ignorant of its better uses, and because a reactionary government insists on banning it. But Transplant is a lot more than a game. It's an entire new way of life! And whether you or the government like it or not, Transplant represents the world of the future.'

The little pusher's eyes glowed. Blaine sat down again.

'There are two basic elements in human affairs,' Joe said sententiously. 'One of them is man's eternal struggle for freedom: Freedom of worship, freedom of press and assembly, freedom to select government – freedom! And the other basic element in human affairs is the efforts of government to withhold freedom from the people.'

Blaine considered this a somewhat simplified view of human affairs. But he continued listening.

'Government,' Joe said, 'withholds freedom for many reasons. For security, for personal profit, for power, or because they feel the people are unready for it. But whatever the reason, the basic facts remain: Man strives for freedom, and government strives to withhold freedom. Transplant is simply one more in a long series of the freedoms that man has aspired to, and that his government feels is not good for him.'

'Sexual freedom?' Blaine asked mockingly.

'No!' Joe cried. 'Not that there's anything wrong with sexual freedom. But Transplant isn't primarily that. Sure, that's how we're pushing it – for propaganda purposes. Because people don't want abstract ideas, Mr. Blaine, and they don't go for cold theory. They want to know what a freedom will *do* for them. We show them a small part of it, and they learn a lot more themselves.'

'What will Transplant do?' Blaine asked.

'Transplant,' Joe said fervently, 'gives man the ability to transcend the limits imposed by his heredity and his environment!'

'Huh?'

'Yes! Transplant lets you exchange knowledge, bodies, talents and skills with anyone who wishes to exchange with you. And plenty do. Most men don't want to perform a single set of skills all their life, no matter how satisfying those skills are. Man is too restless a creature. Musicians want to be engineers, advertising men want to be hunters, sailors want to be writers. But there usually isn't time to acquire and exploit more than one set of skills in a lifetime. And even if there were time, the blind factor of talent is an insurmountable stumbling block. With Transplant, you can get the inborn talents, the skills, the knowledge that you want. Think about it, Mr. Blaine. Why should a man be forced to live out his lifetime in a body he had no part in selecting? It's like telling him he must live with the diseases he's inherited, and mustn't try to cure them. Man must have the freedom to choose the body and talents best suited to his personality needs.'

'If your plan went through,' Blaine said, 'you'd simply have a bunch of neurotics changing bodies every day.'

'The same general argument was raised against the passage of every freedom,' Joe said, his eyes glittering. 'Throughout history it was argued that man didn't have the sense to choose his own religion, or that women didn't have the intelligence to use the vote, or that people couldn't be allowed to elect their own representatives because of the stupid choices they'd make. And of course there are plenty of neurotics around, people who'd louse up heaven itself. But you have a much greater number of people who'd use their freedoms well.'

Joe lowered his voice to a persuasive whisper. 'You must realize, Mr. Blaine, that a man is not his body, for he receives his body accidentally. He is not his skills, for those are frequently born of necessity. He is not his talents, which are produced by heredity and by early environmental factors. He is not the sicknesses to which he may be predisposed, and he is not the environment that shapes him. A man *contains* all these things, but he is greater than their total. He has the power to change his environment, cure his diseases, advance his skills – and, at last, to choose his body and talents! *That* is the next freedom, Mr. Blaine! It's historically inevitable, whether you or I or the government like it or not. For man must have every possible freedom!'

Joe finished his fierce and somewhat incoherent oration red-faced and out of breath. Blaine stared at the little man with new respect. He was looking, he realized, at a genuine revolutionary of the year 2110.

Orc said, 'He's got a point, Tom. Transplant is legal in Sweden and Ceylon, and it doesn't seem to have hurt the moral fibre much.'

'In time,' Joe said, pouring himself a glass of wine, 'the whole world will go Transplant. It's inevitable.'

'Maybe,' Orc said. 'Or maybe they'll invent some new freedom to take its place. Anyhow, Tom, you can see that Transplant has some moral justifications. And it's the only way of saving that body of yours. What do you say?'

'Are you a revolutionary, too?' Blaine asked.

Orc grinned. 'Could be. I guess I'm like the blockade runners during the American Civil War, or the guys who sold guns to Central American revolutionaries. They worked for a profit, but they weren't against social change.'

'Well, well,' Blaine said sardonically. 'And up to now I thought you were just a common criminal.'

'Skip it,' Orc said pleasantly. 'Are you willing to try?'

'Certainly. I'm overwhelmed,' Blaine said. 'I never thought I'd find myself in the advance guard of a social revolution.'

Orc smiled and said, 'Good. Hope it works out for you, Tom. Roll up your sleeve. We'd better get started.'

Blaine rolled up his left sleeve while Orc took a hypodermic from a drawer.

'This is just to knock you out,' Orc explained. 'The Yoga Machine is in the next room. It does the real work. When you come to, you'll be a guest in someone else's mind, and your body will be travelling cross country in deep freeze. They'll be brought together as soon as it's safe.'

'How many minds will I occupy?' Blaine asked. 'And for how long?'

'I don't know how many we'll have to use. As for how long in each, a few seconds, minutes, maybe half an hour. We'll move you along as fast as we can. This isn't a full Transplant, you know. You won't be taking over the body. You'll just be occupying a small portion of its consciousness, as an observer. So stay quiet and act natural. Got that?'

Blaine nodded. 'But how does this Yoga Machine work?'

'It works like Yoga,' Orc said. 'The machine simply does what you could do yourself if you were thoroughly trained in Yoga exercises. It relaxes every muscle and nerve in your body, focuses and calms your mind, helps build up your concentration. When you've reached potential, you're ready to make an astral projection. The machine does that for you, too. It helps you release your hold on the body, which a Yoga adept could do without mechanical assistance. It projects you to the person we've selected, who yields room. Attraction takes care of the rest. You slip in like a stranded fish going back into water.'

'Sounds risky,' Blaine said. 'Suppose I can't get in?'

'Man, you can't *help* but get in! Look, you've heard of demonic possession, haven't you? Guys under the control

172

of so-called demons? The idea runs through most of the world's folklore. Some of the possessed were schizophrenic, of course, and some were downright frauds. But there were a lot of cases of real spiritual invasion, minds taken over by others who had learned the trick of breaking out of their own body and casting into another. The invaders took over with no mechanical help, and against an all-out battle on the part of their victims. In your case you've got the Yoga Machine, and the people are willing to have you in. So why worry?'

'All right,' Blaine said. 'What are the Marquesas like?'

'Beautiful,' Orc said, sliding the needle into Blaine's arm. 'You'll like it there.'

Blaine drifted slowly into unconsciousness, thinking of palm trees, of white surf breaking against a coral reef, and of dark-eyed maidens worshipping a god of stone.

30

There was no sense of awakening, no feeling of transition. Abruptly, like a brilliantly colored slide projected upon a white screen, he was conscious. Suddenly, like a marionette jerked into violent life, he was acting and moving.

He was not completely Thomas Blaine. He was Edgar Dyersen as well. Or he was Blaine within Dyersen, an integral part of Dyersen's body, a segment of Dyersen's mind, viewing the world through Dyersen's rheumy eyes, thinking Dyersen's thoughts, experiencing all the shadowy half-conscious fragments of Dyersen's memories, hopes, fears and desires. And yet he was still Blaine.

Dyersen-Blaine came out of the ploughed field and rested against his wooden fence. He was a farmer, an old-fashioned South Jersey truck farmer, with a minimum of machines which he distrusted anyhow. He was close to seventy and in damn good health. There was still a touch of arthritis in his joints, which the smart young medico in the village had mostly fixed; and his back sometimes gave him trouble before rain. But he considered himself healthy, healthier than most, and good for another twenty years.

Dyersen-Blaine started toward his cottage. His gray workshirt was drenched in acrid sweat, and sweat stained his shapeless levis.

In the distance he heard a dog barking and saw, blurrily, a yellow and brown shape come bounding toward him. (Eyeglasses? No thank you. Doing pretty well with what I got.)

'Hey, Champ! Hey there, boy!'

The dog ran a circle around him, then trotted along beside him. He had something gray in his jaws, a rat or perhaps a piece of meat. Dyersen-Blaine couldn't quite make it out.

He bent down to pat Champ's head . . .

Again there was no sense of transition or of the passage of time. A new slide was simply projected onto the screen, and a new marionette was jerked into life.

Now he was Thompson-Blaine, nineteen years old, lying on his back half dozing on the rough planks of a sailing skiff, the mainsheet and tiller held loosely in one brown hand. To starboard lay the low Eastern shore, and to his port he could see a bit of Baltimore Harbor. The skiff moved easily on the light summer breeze, and water gurgled merrily beneath the forefoot.

Thompson-Blaine rearranged his lanky, tanned body on the planks, squirming around until he had succeeded in propping his feet against the mast. He had been home just a week, after a two-year work and study program on Mars. It had sure been interesting, especially the archaeology and speleology. The sand-farming had gotten dull sometimes, but he had enjoyed driving the harvesting machines.

Now he was home for a two-year accelerated college course. Then he was supposed to return to Mars as a farm manager. That's the way his scholarship read. But they couldn't make him go back if he didn't want to.

Maybe he would. And maybe not.

The girls on Mars were such dedicated types. Tough, capable, and always a little bossy. When he went back – *if* he went back – he'd bring his own wife, not look for one there. Of course there had been Marcia, and she'd really been something. But her whole kibbutz had moved to the South Polar Gap, and she hadn't answered his last three letters. Maybe she hadn't been so much, anyhow.

'Hey, Sandy!'

Thompson-Blaine looked up and saw Eddie Duelitle, sailing his Thistle, waving at him. Languidly Thompson-Blaine waved back. Eddie was only seventeen, had never been off Earth, and wanted to be a spaceliner captain. Huh! Fat chance!

The sun was dipping toward the horizon, and Thompson-Blaine was glad to see it go down. He had a date tonight with Jennifer Hunt. They were going dancing at

Starsling in Baltimore, and Dad was letting him use the heli. Man, how Jennifer had grown in two years! And she had a way of looking at a guy, sort of coy and bold at the same time. No telling what might happen after the dance, in the back seat of the heli. Maybe nothing. But maybe, maybe . . .

Thompson-Blaine sat up and put the tiller over. The skiff came into the wind and tacked over. It was time to return to the yacht basin, then home for dinner, then . . .

The blacksnake whip flicked across his back.

'Get working there, you!'

Piggot-Blaine redoubled his efforts, lifting the heavy pick high in the air and swinging it down into the dusty roadbed. The guard stood nearby, shotgun under his left arm, whip in his right, its lash trailing in the dust. Piggot-Blaine knew every line and pore of that guard's thin, stupid face, knew the downward twist of the tight little mouth, knew the squint of the faded eyes just like he knew his own face.

Just wait, buzzard meat, he silently told the guard. Your time's a-coming. Just wait, wait just a bit.

The guard moved away, walking slowly up and down the line of prisoners laboring under the white Mississippi sun. Piggot-Blaine tried to spit, but couldn't work up enough saliva. He thought, you talk about your fine modern world? Talk about your big old spaceships, your automatic farms, your big fine fat old hereafter? Think that's how it is? Then ask 'em how they build the roads in Quilleg County, Northern Mississippi. They won't tell you, so you better look for yourself and find out. Cause that's the kind of world it *really* is!

Arny, working in front of him, whispered, 'You ready, Otis? You ready for it?'

'I'm a-ready,' Piggot-Blaine whispered, his broad fingers clenching and unclenching on the pick's plastic handle. 'I'm *past* ready, Arny.'

'In a second, then. Watch Jeff.'

Piggot-Blaine's hairy chest swelled expectantly. He

brushed lank brown hair from his eyes and watched Jeff, five men ahead on the chain. Piggot-Blaine waited, his shoulders aching from sunburn. There were callused scars on his ankles from the hoofcuffs, and old seams on his back from earlier whippings. He had a raging thirst in his gut. But no dipperful of water could ever cut that thirst, nothing could, that crazy thirst that brought him in here after he'd dismembered Gainsville's single saloon and killed that stinking old Indian.

Jeff's hand moved. The chained line of prisoners sprang forward. Piggot-Blaine jumped toward the thin-faced guard, his pick swung high, as the guard dropped his whip and fumbled to bring up the shotgun.

'Buzzard meat!' Piggot-Blaine screamed, and brought the pick down fair in the guard's forehead.

'Get the keys!'

Piggot-Blaine grabbed the keys from the dead guard's belt. He heard a shotgun go off, heard a high scream of agony. Anxiously he looked up . . .

Ramirez-Blaine was piloting his heli above the flat Texas plains, heading for El Paso. He was a serious young man and he paid strict attention to his work, coaxing the last knot of speed out of the old heli so he could reach El Paso before Johnson's Hardware Store closed.

He handled the balky rattletrap with care, and only an occasional thought came through his concentration, quick thoughts about the altitude and compass readings, a dance in Guanajuato next week, the price of hides in Ciudad Juárez.

The plain was mottled green and yellow below him. He glanced at his watch, then at the airspeed indicator.

Yes, Ramirez-Blaine thought, he *would* make El Paso before the store closed! He might even have time for a little . . .

Tyler-Blaine wiped his mouth on his sleeve and sopped up the last of the grease gravy on a piece of corn bread. He belched, pushed his chair back from the kitchen table and stood up. With elaborate unconcern he took a cracked bowl from the pantry and filled it with scraps of pork, a few greens, and a big piece of corn bread.

'Ed,' his wife said, 'what are you doing?'

He glanced at her. She was gaunt, tangle-haired, and faded past her years. He looked away, not answering.

'Ed! Tell me, Ed!'

Tyler-Blaine looked at her in annoyance, feeling his ulcer stir at the sound of that sharp, worried voice. Sharpest voice in all California, he told himself, and he'd married it. Sharp voice, sharp nose, sharp elbows and knees, breastless and barren to boot. Legs to support a body, but not for a second's delight. A belly for filling, not for touching. Of all the girls in California he'd doubtless picked the sorriest, just like the damn fool his Uncle Rafe always said he was.

'Where you taking that bowl of food?' she asked.

'Out to feed the dog,' Tyler-Blaine said, moving toward the door.

'We ain't *got* no dog! Oh Ed, don't do it, not tonight!'

'I'm doin' it,' he said, glad of her discomfort.

'Please, not tonight. Let him shift for himself somewhere else. Ed, listen to me! What if the town found out?'

'It's past sundown,' Tyler-Blaine said, standing beside the door with his bowl of food.

'People spy,' she said. 'Ed, if they find out they'll lynch us, you know they will.'

'You'd look mighty spry from the end of a rope,' Tyler-Blaine remarked, opening the door.

'You do it just to spite me!' she cried.

He closed the door behind him. Outside, it was deep twilight. Tyler-Blaine stood in his yard near the unused chicken coop, looking around. The only house near his was the Flannagans', a hundred yards away. But they minded their own business. He waited to make sure none of the town kids were snooping around. Then he walked forward, carefully holding the bowl of food.

He reached the edge of the scraggly woods and set the bowl down. 'It's all right,' he called softly. 'Come out, Uncle Rafe.'

A man crawled out of the woods on all fours. His face was leaden-white, his lips bloodless, his eyes blank and staring, his features coarse and unfinished, like iron before tempering or clay before firing. A long cut across his neck had festered, and his right leg, where the townsfolk had broken it, hung limp and useless.

'Thanks, boy,' said Rafe, Tyler-Blaine's zombie uncle.

The zombie quickly gulped down the contents of the bowl. When he had finished, Tyler-Blaine asked, 'How you feeling, Uncle Rafe?'

'Ain't feeling nothing. This old body's about through. Another couple days, maybe a week, and I'll be off your hands.'

'I'll take care of you,' Tyler-Blaine said, 'just as long as you can stay alive, Uncle Rafe. I wish I could bring you into the house.'

'No,' the zombie said, 'they'd find out. This is risky enough . . . Boy, how's that skinny wife of yours?'

'Just as mean as ever,' Tyler-Blaine sighed.

The zombie made a sound like laughter. 'I warned you, boy, ten years ago I warned you not to marry that gal. Didn't I?'

'You sure did, Uncle Rafe. You was the only one had sense. Sure wish I'd listened to you.'

'Better you had, boy. Well, I'm going back to my shelter.'

'You feel confident, Uncle?' Tyler-Blaine asked anxiously.

'That I do.'

'And you'll try to *die* confident?'

'I will, boy. And I'll get me into that Threshold, never you fear. And when I do, I'll keep my promise. I truly will.'

'Thank you, Uncle Rafe.'

'I'm a man of my word. I'll haunt her, boy, if the good Lord grants me Threshold. First comes that fat doctor that made me this. But then I'll haunt her. I'll haunt her crazy. I'll haunt her 'til she runs the length of the state of California away from you!'

'Thanks, Uncle Rafe.'

The zombie made a sound like laughter and crawled back into the scraggly woods. Tyler-Blaine shivered uncontrollably for a moment, then picked up the empty bowl and walked back to the sagging washboard house . . .

Mariner-Blaine adjusted the strap of her bathing suit so that it clung more snugly to her slim, supple young body. She slipped the air tank over her back, picked up her respirator and walked toward the pressure lock.

'Janice?'

'Yes mother?' she said, turning, her face smooth and expressionless.

'Where are you going, dear?'

'Just out for a swim, Mom. I thought maybe I'd look at the new gardens on Level 12.'

'You aren't by any chance planning to see Tom Leuwin, are you?'

Had her mother *guessed*? Mariner-Blaine smoothed her black hair and said, 'Certainly not.'

'All right,' her mother said, half smiling and obviously not believing her. 'Try to be home early, dear. You know how worried your father gets.'

She stooped and gave her mother a quick kiss, then hurried into the pressure lock. Mother *knew*, she was sure of it! And wasn't stopping her! But then, why should she? After all, she was seventeen, plenty old enough to do anything she wanted. Kids grew up faster these days than they did in Mom's time, though parents didn't seem to realize it. Parents didn't realize very much. They just wanted to sit around and plan out new acres for the farm. Their idea of fun was to listen to some old classic recording, a Bop piece or a Rock 'n' Roll, and follow it with scores and talk about how free and expressionistic their ancestors had been. And sometimes they'd go through big, glossy art books filled with reproductions of 20th century Comic Strips, and talk about the lost art of satire. Their idea of a really Big Night was to go down to the gallery and stare reverently at the collection of *Saturday Evening Post* covers from the Great Period. But all that long-

180

hair stuff bored her. Nuts to art, she liked the sensories.

Mariner-Blaine adjusted her face mask and respirator, put on her flippers and turned the valve. In a few seconds the lock was filled with water. Impatiently she waited until the pressure had equalized with the water outside. Then the lock opened automatically and she shot out.

Her dad's pressure farm was at the hundred-foot level, not far from the mammoth underwater bulk of Hawaii. She turned downward, descending into the green bloom with quick, powerful strokes. Tom would be waiting for her at the coral caves.

The darkness grew as Mariner-Blaine descended. She switched on her headlamp and took a firmer bite on her respirator. Was it true, she wondered, that soon the undersea farmers would be able to grow their own gills? That's what her science teacher said, and maybe it would happen in her own lifetime. How would she look with gills? Mysterious, probably, sleek and strange, a fish goddess.

Besides, she could always cover them with her hair if they weren't becoming.

In the yellow glow of her lamp she saw the coral caves ahead, a red and pink branched labyrinth with cozy, airlocked places deep within, where you could be sure of privacy. And she saw Tom.

Uncertainty flooded her. Gosh, what if she had a baby? Tom had assured her it would be all right, but he was only nineteen. Was she right in doing this? They had talked about it often enough, and she had shocked him with her frankness. But talking and doing were very different things. What would Tom think of her if she said no? Could she make a joke out of it, pretend she'd just been teasing him?

Long and golden, Tom swam beside her toward the caves. He flashed hello in finger talk. A trigger fish swam by, and then a small shark.

What was she going to do? The caves were very near, looming dark and suggestive before them. Tom smiled at her, and she could feel her heart melting . . .

★

Elgin-Blaine sat upright, realizing that he must have dozed off. He was aboard a small motor vessel, sitting in a deck chair with blankets tucked around him. The little ship rolled and pitched in the cross-sea, but overhead the sun was brilliant, and the trade wind carried the diesel smoke away in a wide dark plume.

'You feeling better, Mr. Elgin?'

Elgin-Blaine looked up at a small, bearded man wearing a captain's cap. 'Fine, just fine,' he said.

'We're almost there,' the captain said.

Elgin-Blaine nodded, disoriented, trying to take stock of himself. He thought hard and remembered that he was shorter than average, heavily muscled, barrel chested, broad shouldered, with legs a little short for such a herculean torso, with large and callused hands. There was an old, jagged scar on his shoulder, souvenir of a hunting accident . . .

Elgin and Blaine merged.

Then he realized that he was back at last in his own body. Blaine was his name, and Elgin was the pseudonym under which Carl Orc and Joe must have shipped him.

The long flight was over! His mind and his body were together again!

'We were told you weren't well, sir,' the captain said. 'But you've been in this coma for so long –'

'I'm fine now,' Blaine told him. 'Are we far from the Marquesas?'

'Not far. The island of Nuku Hiva is just a few hours away.'

The captain returned to his wheelhouse. And Blaine thought about the many personalities he had met and mingled with.

He respected the staunch and independent old Dyersen walking slowly back to his cottage, hoped young Sandy Thompson would return to Mars, felt regret for the warped and murderous Piggot, enjoyed his meeting with the serious and upright Juan Ramirez, felt mingled sorrow and contempt for the sly and ineffectual Ed Tyler, prayed for the best for pretty Janice Mariner.

They were with him still. Good or bad, he wished them all well. They were his family now. Distant relatives, cousins and uncles he would never meet again, nieces and nephews upon whose destiny he would brood.

Like all families they were a mixed lot; but they were *his*, and he could never forget them.

'Nuku Hiva in sight!' the captain called.

Blaine saw, on the edge of the horizon, a tiny black dot capped by a white cumulus cloud. He rubbed his forehead vigorously, determined to think no more about his adopted family. There were present realities to deal with. Soon he would be coming to his new home; and that required a little serious thinking.

31

The ship steamed slowly into Taio Hae Bay. The captain, a proud native son, volunteered to Blaine the principal facts about his new home.

The Marquesas Islands, he explained, were composed of two fairly distinct island groups, all of them rugged and mountainous. Once the group had been called the Cannibal Islands, and the Marquesans had been noted for their ability at cutting out a trading ship or massacring a blackbirding schooner. The French had acquired the islands in 1842, and granted them autonomy in 1993. Nuku Hiva was the main island and capital for the group. Its highest peak, Temetiu, was nearly four thousand feet high. Its port city, Taiohae, boasted a population of almost five thousand souls. It was a quiet, easy-going place, the captain said, and it was considered a sort of shrine all over the hurried, bustling South Seas. For here was the last refuge of unspoiled 20th century Polynesia.

Blaine nodded, absorbing little of the captain's lecture, more impressed by the sight of the great dark mountain ahead laced with silver waterfalls, and by the sound of the ocean pounding against the island's granite face.

He decided he was going to like it here.

Soon the ship was docked at the town wharf, and Blaine stepped off to view the town of Taiohae.

He saw a supermarket and three movie theaters, rows of ranch-style houses, many palm trees, some low white stores with plate glass windows, numerous cocktail lounges, dozens of automobiles, a gas station and a traffic light. The sidewalks were filled with people wearing colorful shirts and pressed slacks. All had on sunglasses.

So this was the last refuge of unspoiled 20th century Polynesia, Blaine thought. A Florida town set in the South Seas!

Still, what more could he expect in the year 2110? Ancient Polynesia was as dead as Merrie England or Bourbon France. And 20th century Florida, he remembered, could be very pleasant indeed.

He walked down Main Street, and saw a notice on a building stating that Postmaster Alfred Gray had been appointed Hereafter, Inc. representative for the Marquesas Group. And further on, he came to a small black building with a sign on it that said *Public Suicide Booth*.

Ah, Blaine thought sardonically, modern civilization is encroaching even here! Next thing you know they'll be setting up a Spiritual Switchboard. And where will we be then?

He had reached the end of town. As he started back, a stout, red-faced man hurried up to him.

'Mr. Elgin? Mr. Thomas Elgin?'

'That's me,' Blaine said, with a certain apprehension.

'Terribly sorry I missed you at the dock,' said the red-faced man, mopping his wide and gleaming forehead with a bandanna. 'No excuse, of course. Sheer oversight on my part. The languor of the islands. Inevitable after a while. Oh, I'm Davis, owner of the Point Boatyard. Welcome to Taiohae, Mr. Elgin.'

'Thank you, Mr. Davis,' Blaine said.

'On the contrary. I want to thank *you* again for answering my advertisement,' Davis said. 'I've been needing a Master Boatwright for months. You have no idea! And frankly, I didn't expect to attract a man of your qualifications.'

'Ummm,' Blaine said, surprised and pleased at the thoroughness of Carl Orc's preparations.

'Not many men around with a grounding in 20th century boatbuilding methods,' Davis said sadly. 'Lost art. Have you had a look around the island?'

'Just very briefly,' Blaine said.

'Think you'll want to stay?' Davis asked anxiously. 'You have no idea how hard it is getting a good boatwright to settle down in a quiet little backwater like this. No sooner do they get here, they want to go charging off to the big booming cities like Papeete or Apia. I know wages are higher in places like that, and there's more amusements and society and things. But Taiohae has a charm of its own.'

'I've had my fill of the cities,' Blaine said, smiling. 'I'm not likely to go charging off, Mr. Davis.'

'Good, good!' Davis said. 'Don't bother coming to work for a few days, Mr. Elgin. Rest, take it easy, look around our island. It's the last refuge of primitive Polynesia, you know. Here are the keys to your house. Number one Temetiu Road, straight up the mountain there. Shall I show you the way?'

'I'll find it,' Blaine said. 'Thanks very much, Mr. Davis.'

'Thank *you*, Mr. Elgin. I'll drop in on you tomorrow after you're a bit more settled. Then you can meet some of our townsfolk. In fact, the mayor's wife is giving a party Thursday. Or is it Friday? Anyhow, I'll find out and let you know.'

They shook hands and Blaine started up Temetiu Road, to his new home.

It was a small, freshly painted bungalow with a spectacular view of Nuku Hiva's three southern bays. Blaine admired the sight for a few minutes, then tried the door. It was unlocked, and he walked in.

'It's about time you got here.'

Blaine just stared, not able to believe what he saw.

'Marie!'

She appeared as slim, lovely and cool as ever. But she was nervous. She talked rapidly and avoided meeting his eyes.

'I thought it would be best if I made the final arrangements on the spot,' she said. 'I've been here for two days, waiting for you. You've met Mr. Davis, haven't you? He seems like a very nice little man.'

'Marie –'

'I told him I was your fiancée,' she said. 'I hope you don't mind, Tom. I had to have some excuse for being here. I said I had come out early to surprise you. Mr. Davis was delighted of course, he wants his Master Boatwright to settle here so badly. Do you mind, Tom? We can always say we broke off the engagement and –'

186

Blaine took her in his arms and said, 'I don't want to break off the engagement. I love you, Marie.'

'Oh Tom, Tom, I love you!' She clung to him fiercely for a moment, then stepped back. 'We'd better arrange for a marriage ceremony soon, if you don't mind. They're *very* stuffy and small-townish here; very 20th century, if you know what I mean.'

'I think I know what you mean,' Blaine said.

They looked at each other and burst out laughing.

32

Marie insisted upon staying at the South Seas Motel until a wedding could be arranged. Blaine suggested a quiet ceremony before a justice of the peace; but Marie surprised him by wanting as large a wedding as Taiohae could produce. It was held on Sunday, at the Mayor's house.

Mr. Davis loaned them a little cutter from the boatyard. They set sail at sunrise for a honeymoon cruise to Tahiti.

For Blaine, it had the sensation of a delicious and fleeting dream. They sailed across a sea carved of green jade, and saw the moon, yellow and swollen, quartered by the cutter's shrouds and tangled in its stays. The sun rose out of a long black cloud, reached its zenith and declined, scouring the sea into a gleaming bowl of brass. They anchored in the lagoon at Papeete and saw the mountains of Mooréa flaming in the sunset, more fantastic than the mountains of the Moon. And Blaine remembered a day on the Chesapeake when he had dreamed, *Ah, Raïatea, the mountains of Mooréa, the fresh trade wind . . .*

A continent and an ocean had separated him from Tahiti, and other obstacles besides. But that had been in another century.

They went to Mooréa, rode horses up the slopes and picked the white tiare Tahiti. They returned to their boat anchored in the bay below, and set sail for the Tuamotos.

At last they returned to Taiohae. Marie started housekeeping, and Blaine began to work at the boatyard.

They waited anxiously through the first weeks, scanning the New York papers, wondering what Rex would do. But no word or sign came from the corporation, and they decided that the danger must be past. Still, they read with relief two months later that the Blaine hunt had been called off.

Blaine's job at the boatyard was interesting and varied. The island cutters and ketches limped in with bent shafts or nicked propellers, with planks that had been splintered against a hidden coral head, with sails blown out by a sudden gale. There were underwater craft to be serviced, boats belonging to the nearby undersea pressure farms that used Taiohae as a supply base. And there were dinghies to build, and an occasional schooner.

Blaine handled all practical details with skill and dispatch. As time went by, he started to write a few publicity releases about the yard for the *South Seas Courier*. This brought in more business, which involved more paper work and a greater need for liaison between the Point Boatyard and the small yards to which it farmed out work. Blaine handled this, and took over advertising as well.

His job as Master Boatwright came to bear an uncanny resemblance to his past jobs as junior yacht designer.

But this no longer bothered him. It seemed obvious to him now that nature had intended him to be a junior yacht designer, nothing more nor less. This was his destiny, and he accepted it.

His life fell into a pleasant routine built around the boatyard and the white bungalow, filled with Saturday night movies and the microfilm Sunday *Times*, quick visits to the undersea farms and to other islands in the Marquesas Group, parties at the Mayor's house and poker at the yacht club, brisk sails across Comptroller Bay and moonlight swimming on Temuoa Beach. Blaine began to think that his life had taken its final and definitive form.

Then, nearly four months after he had come to Taiohae, the pattern changed again.

One morning like any other morning Blaine woke up, ate his breakfast, kissed his wife goodbye and went down to the boatyard. There was a fat, round-bilged ketch on the ways, a Tuamotan boat that had gauged wrong trying to shoot a narrow pass under sail, and had been tide-set against a foam-splattered granite wall before the crew could start the

189

engine. Six frames needed sistering, and a few planks had to be replaced. Perhaps they could finish it in a week.

Blaine was looking over the ketch when Mr. Davis came over.

'Say Tom,' the owner said, 'there was a fellow around here just a little while ago looking for you. Did you see him?'

'No,' Blaine said. 'Who was it?'

'A mainlander,' Davis said, frowning. 'Just off the steamer this morning. I told him you weren't here yet and he said he'd see you at your house.'

'What did he look like?' Blaine asked, feeling his stomach muscles tighten.

Davis frowned more deeply. 'Well, that's the funny part of it. He was about your height, thin, and very tanned. Had a full beard and sideburns. You don't see that much any more. And he stank of shaving lotion.'

'Sounds peculiar,' Blaine said.

'Very peculiar. I'll swear his beard wasn't real.'

'No?'

'It looked like a fake. Everything about him looked fake. And he limped pretty bad.'

'Did he leave a name?'

'Said his name was Smith. Tom, where are you going?'

'I have to go home right now,' Blaine said. 'I'll try to explain later.'

He hurried away. Smith must have found out who he was and what the connection was between them. And, exactly as he had promised, the zombie had come visiting.

33

When he told Marie, she went at once to a closet and took down their suitcases. She carried them into the bedroom and began flinging clothes into them.

'What are you doing?' Blaine asked.

'Packing.'

'So I see. But why?'

'Because we're getting out of here.'

'What are you talking about? We live here!'

'Not any more,' she said. 'Not with that damned Smith around. Tom, he means trouble.'

'I'm sure he does,' Blaine said. 'But that's no reason to run. Stop packing a minute and listen! What do you think he can do to me?'

'We're not going to stay and find out,' she said.

She continued to shove clothes into the suitcase until Blaine grabbed her wrists.

'Calm down,' he told her. 'I'm not going to run from Smith.'

'But it's the only sensible thing to do,' Marie said. 'He's trouble, but he can't live much longer. Just a few more months, weeks maybe, and he'll be dead. He should have died long before now, that horrible zombie! Tom, let's go!'

'Have you gone crazy or something?' Blaine asked. 'Whatever he wants, I can handle it.'

'I've heard you say that before,' Marie said.

'Things were different then.'

'They're different now! Tom, we could borrow the cutter again, Mr. Davis would understand, and we could go to –'

'No! I'm damned if I'll run from him! Maybe you've forgotten, Marie, Smith saved my life.'

'But what did he save it *for*?' she wailed. 'Tom, I'm warning you! You mustn't see him, not if he remembers!'

191

'Wait a minute,' Blaine said slowly. 'Is there something you know? Something I don't?'

She grew immediately calm. 'Of course not.'

'Marie, are you telling me the truth?'

'Yes, darling. But I'm frightened of Smith. Please Tom, humor me this once, let's go away.'

'I won't run another step from anyone,' Blaine said. 'I live here. And that's the end of it.'

Marie sat down, looking suddenly exhausted. 'All right, dear. Do what you think is best.'

'That's better,' Blaine said. 'It'll turn out all right.'

'Of course it will,' Marie said.

Blaine put the suitcases back and hung up the clothes. Then he sat down to wait. He was physically calm. But in memory he had returned to the underground, had passed again through the ornate door covered with Egyptian hieroglyphics and Chinese ideograms, into the vast marble-pillared Palace of Death with its gold and bronze coffin. And heard again Reilly's screaming voice speak through a silvery mist:

'There are things you can't see, Blaine, but *I* see them. Your time on Earth will be short, very short, painfully short. Those you trust will betray you, those you hate will conquer you. You will die, Blaine, not in years but soon, sooner than you could believe. You'll be betrayed, and you'll die by your own hand.'

That mad old man! Blaine shivered slightly and looked at Marie. She sat with downcast eyes, waiting. So he waited, too.

After a while there was a soft knock at the door.

'Come in,' Blaine said to whoever was outside.

34

Blaine recognized Smith immediately, even with false beard, sideburns and tan stage makeup. The zombie came in, limping, bringing with him a faint odor of decay imperfectly masked by a powerful shaving lotion.

'Excuse the disguise,' Smith said. 'It isn't intended to deceive you, or anyone. I wear it because my face is no longer presentable.'

'You've come a long way,' Blaine said.

'Yes, quite far,' Smith agreed, 'and through difficulties I won't bore you by relating. But I got here, that's the important thing.'

'Why did you come?'

'Because I know who I am,' Smith said.

'And you think it concerns me?'

'Yes.'

'I can't imagine how,' Blaine said grimly. 'But let's hear it.'

Marie said, 'Wait a minute. Smith, you've been after him since he came into this world. He's never had a moment's peace. Can't you just accept things as they are? Can't you just go and die quietly somewhere?'

'Not without telling him first,' Smith said.

'Come on, let's hear it,' Blaine said.

Smith said, 'My name is James Olin Robinson.'

'Never heard of you,' Blaine said after a moment's thought.

'Of course not.'

'Have we ever met before that time in the Rex building?'

'Not formally.'

'But we met?'

'Briefly.'

'All right, James Olin Robinson, tell me about it. When did we meet?'

'It was quite brief,' Robinson said. 'We glimpsed each other for a fraction of a second, then saw no more. It happened late one night in 1958, on a lonely highway, you in your car and me in mine.'

'You were driving the car I had the accident with?'

'Yes. If you can call it an accident.'

'But it was! It was completely accidental!'

'If that's true, I have no further business here,' Robinson said. 'But Blaine, I *know* it was not an accident. It was murder. Ask your wife.'

Blaine looked at his wife sitting in a corner of the couch. Her face was waxen. She seemed drained of vitality. Her gaze seemed to turn inward and not enjoy what it saw there. Blaine wondered if she was staring at the ghost of some ancient guilt, long buried, long quickening, now come to term with the appearance of the bearded Robinson.

Watching her, he slowly began piecing things together.

'Marie,' he said, 'what about that night in 1958? How did you know I was going to smash up my car?'

She said, 'There are statistical prediction methods we use, valence factors . . .' Her voice trailed away.

'Or did you *make* me smash up my car?' Blaine asked. 'Did you produce the accident when you wanted it, in order to snatch me into the future for your advertising campaign?'

Marie didn't answer. And Blaine thought hard about the manner of his dying.

He had been driving over a straight, empty highway, his headlights probing ahead, the darkness receding endlessly before him . . . His car swerved freakishly, violently, toward the oncoming headlights . . . He twisted hard on the steering wheel. It wouldn't turn . . . The steering wheel came free and spun in his hands, and the engine wailed . . .

'By God, you made me have that accident!' Blaine shouted at his wife. 'You and Rex Power Systems, you forced my car into a swerve! Look at me and answer! Isn't it true?'

'All right!' she said. 'But we didn't mean to kill *him*. Robinson just happened to be in the way. I'm sorry about that.'

Blaine said, 'You've known all along who he was.'

'I've suspected.'

'And never told me.' Blaine paced up and down the room. 'Marie! Damn you, you killed me!'

'I didn't, Tom! Not really. I took you from 1958 into our time. I gave you a different body. But I didn't really kill you.'

'You simply killed *me*,' Robinson said.

With an effort Marie turned from her inner gaze and looked at him. 'I'm afraid I was responsible for your death, Mr. Robinson, although not intentionally. Your body must have died at the same time as Tom's. The Rex Power System that snatched him into the future pulled you along, too. Then you took over Reilly's host.'

'A very poor exchange for my former body,' Robinson said.

'I'm sure it was. But what do you want? What can I do? The hereafter –'

'I don't want it,' Robinson said. 'I haven't had a chance on the Earth yet.'

'How old were you at the time of the accident?' Blaine asked.

'Nineteen.'

Blaine nodded sadly.

'I'm not ready for the hereafter,' Robinson said. 'I want to travel, do things, see things. I want to find out what kind of a man I am. I want to live! Do you know, I've never really known a woman! I'd exchange immortality for ten good years on Earth.'

Robinson hesitated a moment, then said, 'I want a body. I want a man's good body that I can live in. Not this dead thing which I wear. Blaine, your wife killed my former body.'

Blaine said, 'You want mine?'

'If you think it's fair,' Robinson said.

'Now wait just a minute!' Marie cried. Color had returned to her face. With her confession, she seemed to have freed herself from the grip of the ancient evil in her mind, to have come back to wrestle again with life.

'Robinson,' she said. 'You can't ask that from him. He didn't have anything to do with your death. It was my fault, and I'm sorry. You don't want a woman's body, do you? I wouldn't give you mine, anyhow. What's done is done! Get out of here!'

Robinson ignored her and looked at Blaine. 'I always knew it was you, Blaine. When I knew nothing else, I knew it was you. I watched over you, Blaine, I saved your life.'

'Yes, you did,' Blaine said quietly.

'*So what!*' Marie screamed. 'So he saved your life. That doesn't mean he owns it! One doesn't save a life and expect it to be forfeited upon request. Tom, don't listen to him!'

Robinson said, 'I have no means or intention of forcing you, Blaine. You will decide what you think is right, and I will abide by it. You will remember *everything*.'

Blaine looked at the zombie almost with affection. 'So there's more to it. Much more. Isn't there, Robinson?'

Robinson nodded, his eyes fixed on Blaine's face.

'But how did you know?' Blaine asked. 'How could you possibly know?'

'Because I understand you. I've made you my lifetime work. My life has revolved around you. I've thought about nothing but you. And the better I knew you, Blaine, the more certain I was about this.'

'Perhaps,' Blaine said.

Marie said, 'What on earth are you talking about? What more? What more could there be?'

'I have to think about this,' Blaine said. 'I have to remember. Robinson, please wait outside for a little while.'

'Certainly,' the zombie said, and left immediately.

Blaine waved Marie into silence. He sat down and buried his head in his hands. Now he had to remember something he would rather not think about. Now, once and for all, he had to trace it back and understand it.

Etched sharp in his mind still were the words Reilly had screamed at him in the Palace of Death: 'You're responsible! You killed me with your evil murdering mind! Yes *you*, you hideous thing from the past, you damned monster!

Everything shuns you except your friend the dead man! Why aren't *you* dead, murderer?'

Had Reilly known?

He remembered Sammy Jones saying to him after the hunt: 'Tom, you're a natural-born killer. There's nothing else for you.'

Had Sammy guessed?

And now the most important thing of all. That most significant moment of his life – the time of his death on a night in 1958. Vividly he remembered:

The steering wheel was working again, but Blaine ignored it, filled with a sudden fierce exultancy, a lightning switch of mood that welcomed the smash, lusted for it, and for pain and cruelty and death . . .

Blaine shuddered convulsively as he relived the moment he had wanted to forget – the moment when he might have avoided catastrophe, but had preferred to kill.

He lifted his head and looked at his wife. He said, 'I killed him. That's what Robinson knew. And now I know it, too.'

35

Carefully he explained it all to Marie. She refused at first to believe him.

'It was so far back, Tom! How can you be sure of what happened?'

'I'm sure,' Blaine said. 'I don't think anyone could forget the way they died. I remember mine very well. *That* was how I died.'

'Still, you can't call yourself a murderer because of one moment, one fraction of a second —'

'How long does it take to shoot a bullet or to drive in a knife?' Blaine asked. 'A fraction of a second! That's how long it takes to become a murderer.'

'But Tom, you had no motive!'

Blaine shook his head. 'It's true that I didn't kill for gain or revenge. But then, I'm not that kind of murderer. That kind is relatively rare. I'm the grass-roots variety, the ordinary average guy with a little of everything in his makeup, including murder. I killed because, in that moment, I had the *opportunity*. My special opportunity, a unique interlocking of events, moods, train of thought, humidity, temperature, and Lord knows what else, which might not have come up again in two lifetimes.'

'But you're not to blame!' Marie said. 'It would never have happened if Rex Power Systems and I hadn't created that special opportunity for you.'

'Yes. But I seized the opportunity,' Blaine said, 'seized it and performed a cold-blooded murder just for fun, because I knew I could never be caught at it. *My* murder.'

'Well . . . Our murder,' she said.

'Yes.'

'All right, we're murderers,' Marie said calmly. 'Accept it, Tom. Don't get mushy-minded about it. We've killed once, we can kill again.'

198

'Never,' Blaine said.

'He's almost finished! I swear to you, Tom, there's not a month of life in him. He's almost played out. One blow and he's done for. One push.'

'I'm not that kind of murderer,' Blaine said.

'Will you let me do it?'

'I'm not that kind, either.'

'You idiot! Then just do nothing! Wait. A month, no more than that, and he's finished. You can wait a month, Tom –'

'More murder,' Blaine said wearily.

'Tom! You're not going to give him your body! What about our life together?'

'Do you think we could go on after this?' Blaine asked. 'I couldn't. Now stop arguing with me. I don't know if I'd do this if there weren't a hereafter. Quite probably I wouldn't. But there *is* a hereafter. I'd like to go there with my accounts as straight as possible, all bills paid in full, all restitutions made. If this were my only existence, I'd cling to it with everything I've got. But it isn't! Can you understand that?'

'Yes, of course,' Marie said unhappily.

'Frankly, I'm getting pretty curious about this afterlife. I want to see it. And there's one thing more.'

'What's that?'

Marie's shoulders were trembling, so Blaine put his arm around her. He was thinking back to the conversation he had had with Hull, the elegant and aristocratic Quarry.

Hull had said: 'We follow Nietzsche's dictum – to die at the right time! Intelligent people don't clutch at the last shreds of life like drowning men clinging to a bit of board. They know that the body's life is only an infinitesimal portion of man's total existence. Why shouldn't those bright pupils skip a grade or two of school?'

Blaine remembered how strange, dark, atavistic and noble Hull's lordly selection of death had seemed. Pretentious, of course; but then, life itself was a pretension in the vast universe of unliving matter. Hull had seemed like an ancient Japanese nobleman kneeling to perform the ceremonial act of hara-kiri, and emphasizing the importance of life in the very selection of death.

And Hull had said: 'The deed of dying transcends class and breeding. It is every man's patent of nobility, his summons from the king, his knightly adventure. And how he acquits himself in that lonely and perilous enterprise is his true measure as a man.'

Marie broke into his reverie, asking, 'What was that one thing more?'

'Oh.' Blaine thought for a moment. 'I just wanted to say that I guess some of the attitudes of the 22nd century have rubbed off on me. Especially the aristocratic ones.' He grinned and kissed her. 'But of course, I always had good taste.'

36

Blaine opened the door of the cottage. 'Robinson,' he said, 'come with me to the Suicide Booth. I'm giving you my body.'

'I expected no less of you, Tom,' the zombie said.

'Then let's go.'

Together they went slowly down the mountainside. Marie watched them from a window for a few seconds, then started down after them.

They stopped at the door to the Suicide Booth. Blaine said, 'Do you think you can take over all right?'

'I'm sure of it,' Robinson said. 'Tom, I'm grateful for this. I'll use your body well.'

'It's not mine, really,' Blaine said. 'Belonged to a fellow named Kranch. But I've grown fond of it. You'll get used to its habits. Just remind it once in a while who's boss. Sometimes it wants to go hunting.'

'I think I'll like that,' Robinson said.

'Yes, I suppose you would. Well, good luck.'

'Good luck to you, Tom.'

Marie came up and kissed Blaine goodbye with icy lips. Blaine said, 'What will you do?'

She shrugged her shoulders. 'I don't know. I feel so numb . . . Tom, must you?'

'I must,' Blaine said.

He looked around once more at the palm trees whispering under the sun, the blue expanse of the sea, and the great dark mountain above him cut with silver waterfalls. Then he turned and entered the Suicide Booth, and closed the door behind him.

There were no windows, no furniture except a single chair. The instructions posted on one wall were very simple. You just sat down, and, at your leisure, closed the switch upon the right arm. You would then die, quickly and painlessly, and your body would be left intact for the next inhabitant.

Blaine sat down, made sure of the location of the switch and leaned back, his eyes closed.

He thought again about the first time he died, and wished it had been more interesting. By rights he should have rectified the error this time, and gone down like Hull, hunted fiercely across a mountain ledge at sundown. Why couldn't it have been like that? Why couldn't death have come while he was battling a typhoon, meeting a tiger's charge, or climbing Mount Everest? Why, again, would his death be so tame, so commonplace, so ordinary?

But then, why had he never really designed yachts?

An enterprising death, he realized again, would be out of character for him. Undoubtedly he was meant to die in just this quick, commonplace, painless way. And all his life in the future must have gone into the forming and shaping of this death – a vague indication when Reilly died, a fair certainty in the Palace of Death, an implacable destiny when he settled in Taiohae.

Still, no matter how ordinary, one's death is the most interesting event of one's life. Blaine looked forward eagerly to his.

He had no complaint to make. Although he had lived in the future little over a year, he had gained its greatest prize – the hereafter! He felt again what he had experienced after leaving the Hereafter Building – release from the heavy, sodden, constant, unconscious fear of death that subtly weighed every action and permeated every movement. No man of his own age could live without the shadow that crept down the corridors of his mind like some grisly tapeworm, the ghost that haunted nights and days, the croucher behind corners, the shape behind doors, the unseen guest at every banquet, the unidentified figure in every landscape, always present, always waiting –

No more!

For now the ancient enemy was defeated. And men no longer died; they *moved on*!

But he had gained even more than an afterlife. He had

managed to squeeze and compress an entire lifetime into that year.

He had been born in a white room with dazzling lights and a doctor's bearded face above him, and a motherly nurse to feed him while he listened, alarmed, to the babble of strange tongues. He had ventured early into the world, raw and uneducated, and had stared at the oriental marvel of New York, and allowed a straight-eyed fast-talking stranger to make a fool and nearly a corpse of him, until wiser heads rescued him from his folly and soothed his pain. Clothed in his fine, strong, mysterious body he had ventured out again, wiser this time, and had moved as an equal among men equipped with glittering weapons in the pursuit of danger and honor. And he had lived through that folly, too, and still older, had chosen an honorable occupation. But certain dark omens present at his birth finally reached fruition, and he had to flee his homeland and run to the farthest corner of the Earth. Yet he still managed to acquire a family on the way; a family with certain skeletons in the closet, but his all the same. In the fullness of manhood he had come to a land he loved, taken a wife, and, on his honeymoon, seen the mountains of Mooréa flaming in the sunset. He had settled down to spend his declining months in peace and useful labor, and in fond recollection of the wonders he had seen. And so he had spent them, honored and respected by all.

It was sufficient. Blaine turned the switch.

37

'Where am I? Who am I? What am I?'

No answer.

'I remember. I am Thomas Blaine, and I have just died. I am now in the Threshold, a very real and completely indescribable place. I sense Earth. And ahead, I sense the hereafter.'

'Tom –'

'Marie!'

'Yes.'

'But how could you – I didn't think –'

'Well, perhaps in some ways I wasn't a very good wife, Tom. But I was always a faithful one, and I did what I did for you. I love you, Tom. Of course I would follow.'

'Marie, this makes me very happy.'

'I'm glad.'

'Shall we go on?'

'Where, Tom?'

'Into the hereafter.'

'Tom, I'm frightened. Couldn't we just stay right here for a while?'

'It'll be all right. Come with me.'

'Oh, Tom! What if they separate us? What will it be like? I don't think I'm going to like it. I'm afraid it's going to be terribly strange and ghostly and horrible.'

'Marie, don't worry. I've been a junior yacht designer three times in two lifetimes. It's my destiny! Surely it can't end here!'

'All right. I'm ready now, Tom. Let's go.'